HYBRID

A PARANORMAL WOMEN'S FICTION NOVEL

IMMORTAL WEST
BOOK 2

L.A. BORUFF

KERRY ADRIENNE

© Copyright 2022 L.A. Boruff & Kerry Adrienne

Cover by Jacqueline Sweet

Formatting by L.A. Boruff

All rights reserved under the International and Pan-American Copyright Conventions. No part of this book may be reproduced or transmitted in any form or by any means, electronic or mechanical, including photocopying, recording, or by any information storage and retrieval system, without permission in writing from the publisher.

This is a work of fiction. Names, places, characters and incidents are either the product of the author's imagination or are used fictitiously, and any resemblance to any actual persons, living or dead, organizations, events or locales is entirely coincidental.

Warning: the unauthorized reproduction or distribution of this copyrighted work is illegal. Criminal copyright infringement, including infringement without monetary gain, is investigated by the FBI and is punishable by up to 5 years in prison and a fine of $250,000.

Created with Vellum

For anyone who, like us, needs to escape out of this world and into an alternate universe.

1

CLAIRE

I *won* it.

A low-level hum of piano music, laughter, feet tapping, and glasses clinking soothed my nerves.

The Dusty Bunny was my saloon now. And I'd fight to the death to protect it. Not just because it was a saloon that made me a fair bit of coin, but because it was useful. It'd help me form the connections I needed to stop the high fae from tricking humans and turning them into their breeding stock love slaves.

Although there wasn't much love involved.

I'd been lured to The Rift under false pretense, but that didn't mean I'd allow it to happen to other humans. My uncle had taught me better than that.

I'd stand up for what was right, even if it wasn't directly affecting me at the time.

If more people stood up, the world might not be in such a mess—my world or The Rift, take your pick. Selfishness and greed caused more problems than could be fended off with a sharp stick, and I'd fight for what was right any way I could. If that meant making coin and using it to save others, well then, I could think of no better calling.

I leaned forward in my chair and drummed my fingers on the table. I wasn't impatient, I was making sure I could still feel my fingertips. If they were getting numb, I knew I needed to slow the drinks. Uncle Silas had taught me that trick. I could feel the rough wood just fine, but it was a good confirmation that I had things under control.

A belt of laughter roared up from the corner in the back and I glanced over to make sure everything was all right. One of the younger Riders was telling a tale and either his story was funny, or the ale was warming up the crowd too much. Either way, nothing was amiss. Let 'em talk. He didn't know enough to cause any trouble.

I tugged at my silky overskirt, trying for the fiftieth time tonight to get it to sit right around my waist. The corset underneath fit well, but the whole package was well more than I was used to wearing. I'd changed my manner of dress to match the saloon girls that worked here, but the truth was I didn't truly fit in. There was no disguising that I was more comfortable upright than on my back, that dancing with strangers didn't interest me, and I could get my own drinks without selling myself to a stranger for a glass of ale. And although I wore dresses fine, the slippery shiny ones expected here in the saloon gave me fits twisting and slipping with every movement.

Still, I needed to blend in a bit while I planned my next move and figured out how to shut down The Rift entirely. And though the role of women was a bit different in The Rift, the place still relied on some submissive roles for women. Maybe it was a bit better than my Boston, but it was a trade-off.

Not that I judged any of the ladies who worked in the saloon, whether they chose to work in the world's oldest profession or as one of my spies or both. Each of the women worked by choice, and many of them had chosen to follow me here after they'd been freed from the Fae King. I'd given them that choice. A few others had stayed after Donley signed over the saloon.

All now enjoyed lives where they made their own decisions, unlike before I had arrived in The

Rift, and that made me happy. I did have to make money, however, and more money than slinging drinks would allow. Many women had ended up in The Rift alone, stolen from their human homes, and they needed jobs and a place to stay. The Dusty Bunny rented rooms in exchange for protection and a clean and safe working environment. Everyone around knew that the punishment for crossing the line with one of my girls was death, so the saloon rarely had a vacant room for rent.

I pretended to sip my drink and used the moment to scan the bar. The nights when I waited on Riders to return with information were always tense. Not only because the information was sensitive, but because if they were followed, the entire town could be discovered. Any breach of the magical wards would mean death for many, if not all of us.

Around the bar were card games, flirting couples and threesomes, drinking groups, banter, and silliness... I didn't see any problems. Everything looked normal, though my definition of normal had certainly changed since I'd hopped the train from Chicago, thinking I was riding to meet my husband in the American West.

I set my glass down and took a deep breath. I'd

nearly mastered appearing completely calm despite being nervous.

So far, so good. I gave a nod and a smile to a pair of half-drunk young patrons as they headed toward the door. Neither could have been more than eighteen or nineteen, and the blush of youth combined with the ruddy cheeks from too much whisky made them look like consumptives. I knew they weren't sick. In fact, I hadn't heard of a single case of consumption in The Rift so far.

"Evening, Miss Lowell." One of the pair tried to tip his hat and wobbled on unsteady feet, nearly toppling into me.

His friend caught him by the arm and set him straight, shooting me a big smile and a wave of his other hand.

"Evening." I kept my tone flat, knowing that I had to be careful not to send any mixed signals to tipsy men. Not that I couldn't handle them, because I certainly could. I just didn't want to be bothered with the hassle they often caused. I had much better and more important things to do with my time than deal with a soused goose who thought I took a shine to him.

Especially the very young ones and the very old ones.

The men scrambled out the door and I looked away. As long as they weren't bothering anyone, I didn't need to worry about them causing any more trouble than outdrinking the coin they were carrying, and they wouldn't be the only men with a small tab at the saloon.

An old upright piano sat in the corner with Mable plinking out notes that twanged a little more out of tune with every tickle of the ivory. I kept hoping she'd learn a new song or three, but since she didn't charge for her performances, I let her play whatever she wanted. Her tip jar filled up each night and she had plenty of drinks sent her way, so who was I to say she needed a new song anyway?

I wasn't running a concert hall.

I finished off my drink in one gulp and pushed the glass to the center of the table. When would they get back? Night like this, the time passed as slow as molasses on a cold spring day. I took a deep breath to tamp down the anxiety that kept flaring in my gut.

Sarabeth slung half-pint glasses down the bar's scarred wood top, alcohol spilling and sloshing out of the schooners, and Lola worked the floor, her corset top cut low and bosom heaving. She was a pro at keeping the men interested, and more pairs of eyes followed her than most of the other girls.

Toward the back of the saloon, three individual poker games moved along. In one corner, at the largest table, the Hadley boys played with vampires named Roebuck and Dave. They were all regulars, former muscle for the Fae King, but now they were *my* contacts, men I'd put my trust in to keep me informed. The other games and other players didn't matter. They kept buying drinks, so I didn't care how long they kept the seats warm. As long as there was no trouble, I was happy to provide a gathering place for misfits, hard workers, and loners alike.

Better to have them where I could watch them than to wonder what they were up to. Besides, all my girls listened for any information that might help me defeat the Fae King.

Shaleena, one of the witches who traveled around The Rift and re-warded towns like Nobody and others so the Fae King couldn't locate them, sat at the table across from mine, hands wrapped around a cup of hot tea. She stared at the wall, but her mind was elsewhere.

I had just been joined by a group of male customers who'd come in to drink with the new owner.

Me. I straightened in my chair.

Glasses clinked, men spoke, and women giggled

all around us. The air was scented with cigar smoke and stale ale, and the saloon was like a hive of bees on a warm summer's halfmoon.

Such was a Tuesday night at The Dusty Bunny.

Shaleena's features drooped and she yawned. She must have come from a recent warding. I didn't really understand how her magic worked to protect the towns, but it did, and I was grateful for her services. The witches saved a lot of lives, and they risked themselves to do it. Though I offered for her to drink free, she rarely drank anything stronger than herbal tea.

As if sensing me staring, she lifted her chin and smiled. Her eyes, a deep blue, almost purple color, glowed briefly. She was beautiful, with long black hair pulled up in fancy braids and plaits that looped and knotted in a magical coif, and a sinewy body that twisted in a becoming way no matter the volume of cloth that tried to hide it. Men tripped over themselves to win her favor, but her gaze always fell on the fairer sex.

I returned her smile.

Her presence was a welcome one in The Dusty Bunny. I was always on the lookout for shady bad apples who might give away the location of the town of Nobody to the Fae King. The markers that indicated where the town lay had to be constantly moved and sometimes re-warded, and I liked knowing she was keeping an eye on the security of our wards.

I didn't trust very many on this side of The Rift, but Shaleena had proved herself more than once, and who didn't want an Ace-high witch on their side of the rainbow?

We're not in Massachusetts anymore, Claire. I patted my derringer tucked in my stocking top. One day, I'd be less prone to stressing about who might walk through the saloon door, but today was not that day.

The barmaid delivered another round of drinks and before he could down his, Tommy Godwin toppled off the side of his chair onto the wooden floor with a thump and a holler. The old wooden plank floor was coated with a layer of sawdust and another of grime and when Tommy managed to stand—not straight by any stretch of the word—one of Donley's former girls, Alma, took pity and brushed the dirt off him.

He could've used a dip in the river with some soap or a bath in one of the rooms upstairs instead. Even as soused as he already was, somehow Tommy held onto the back of the chair, spun it, and ended up straddling it, still listing, but mostly straight.

"You alright?" Alma spoke loudly, cupping her hands and leaning toward him. "Haven't seen you full as a tick in a long time. Least since last week."

The men and ladies around laughed and even Shaleena grinned. Alma clapped Tommy on the back, and he leaned forward, head in his hands and elbows on the table.

"I'm fine," he drawled.

His mount of the chair was rather impressive yet was the kind of thing no one gave a second gander. Men in the saloon fell from chairs. It was what they did. Tommy Godwin, more than most, but he drank twice as much as every man in the room, so it stood to reason he'd fall the most, being human and all.

Alma's poking fun was just that, poking fun.

I'd matched Tommy drink for drink, and I was still upright. Not because I had a greater tolerance for alcohol, because biology was biology, but I could handle my liquor. I'd been drinking with my uncle since I was ten. Mainly though, I was doing better than ol' Tommy because I asked the barmaid to mix my drinks halfsies with water and with more and more water as the night wore on.

Secret of the trade, and I learned quick. Besides, I had to keep my wits about me.

A couple of the girls sashayed past me, and

Millie dragged a finger across Wyatt's collar, just under his chin where the skin of his neck was tanned and bare. He smiled, and she played coy for a second, then crooked her finger. My girls had grown much bolder in the time I'd known them.

Maybe because I was bold? I loved the thought that they gained confidence from me, or at least felt more comfortable showing it. It was probable since I let them choose their jobs and their customers, declining whoever they didn't want to attend to. Also, unlike Donley, they didn't have to attend to anyone if they didn't want to and I didn't have a hand in their pocket or a nose in their business.

If any man came in with the wrong idea, or hurt one of my girls, he'd have me to answer to. Same for my male employees. I wouldn't tolerate abuse.

Charlotte and Scarlett, blonde-haired, blue-eyed twins who were customer favorites, had been doing shots at the bar before walking over to sit with us. Charlotte was interested in one of the guys and Scarlett had a soft spot for Tommy.

I would've stayed and chatted and had a few more drinks with the group, but one of the girls bent over to whisper in my ear. "Miss Claire, the Riders are back."

Perfect. My heart raced, but I kept my composure solid and steady.

When I finished my drink, knowing they'd wait for me, I bade my nearly comatose drinking companions farewell. "Watch Tommy. Last week he busted his face on the floor." The words were meant for Scarlett, but Charlotte nodded.

I made my way to my office, through the stench of ale and smoke and men. The piano was quiet for the moment but the melody of glasses hitting the bar and tables kept the rhythm of the saloon going. Somewhere back in the back, one of the poker games was kicking up a row.

The hallway to my office was dim and cooler than the saloon, and I paused for a breath. I'd wished for a change in my life when I'd boarded the train west, and I guess I couldn't complain because I'd certainly gotten more than I'd wished for. The whole kit and caboodle was more than I ever could have imagined, and yet I knew I could handle it.

In an odd way, everything felt like it was meant to be—though I'd never have been able to foresee just how much going west was going to change my life. I leaned against the wood paneled wall, fingertips grazing the smooth, cool surface.

Had the Riders found out anything important?

Several of the girls waited in my office for news of how the latest mission had gone. I'd sent the Riders to continue setting up a secret information-gathering service in some of the other hidden settlements. I didn't know a lot about the other communities, but they were there, and these Riders knew where to find them since they already carried messages and supplies between the towns and villages hidden in The Rift. They'd been instructed to talk up the idea of banding together, protecting one another, working for a common cause.

Many of the girls helped gather information. Some of those traveling through spoke of other settlements and while everyone did what they could to not raise suspicions, sometimes it was unavoidable. The Riders handled that, too, if they were around. Otherwise, I took care of it myself.

Same as I took care of Donley—the former owner of the Dusty Bunny. But I didn't talk about that anymore, either.

Certain things didn't need to be said. Not here, or anywhere else, because while I had my own spies, so did the Fae King and Donley had been one of his men. There would be some retribution demanded and I wasn't looking forward to that debt coming due.

I had an objective, and I wasn't letting anyone, or anything, come between me and my goal.

I opened the door and went into my office, which was a fine sight nicer than when it was Donley's. I stood straight, making sure I conveyed to the girls that I had everything under control. That there was nothing to worry about. I sent out the girls who'd been waiting for me and had just taken the seat behind my desk when Blake Rider walked in.

He didn't generally wait to be invited, but walked right on in. Today was no different. Not that I minded.

"I sent your letter off." He spoke without inflection.

"Thank you." I gave him a quick nod and definitely not a full glance. I wondered where the other Riders were but waited on him to speak.

He set an envelope on the stained leather blotter in front of me. My uncle's smooth, neat handwriting smeared across the front. "Sorry. It was raining in St. Louis. Some of the mail got wet."

Blake was the reason I was beyond The Rift in the first place. He'd been hired by Donley to deliver me as a new love slave of the Fae King. I'd thought I was traveling to meet a fine gentleman from the Utah territory who'd been looking for a wife and had offered big money to lure one, money I'd needed to help Uncle Silas, but it had all been a ruse and Blake had known the whole time.

And yet he brought me to The Rift anyway. While I wasn't quite ready to admit to him that I'd forgiven him, despite the fact I didn't blame him anymore, I accepted his help.

I needed it.

As one of the Riders, he was often traveling around The Rift carrying supplies and information and trying to stay ahead of the fae. Recently, he took up going back and forth through The Rift, delivering letters to and from my uncle. As a vampire, he was able to travel more freely than most, but he didn't have to do it. He was risking quite a lot for my sake, and I appreciated it, even if I dealt with him harshly for bringing me to be a slave in the first place.

"Thank you. Anything else?" I waved the letter, tone curt, eyes hooded so he wouldn't see that I had, in fact, forgiven him. I kept my feelings for Blake, things I didn't want to think about, hidden, buried so deep even I wasn't sure they were there until moments like these when he was bigger than life in my office.

"The Riders will be here in a few. They're tending to the horses first."

"Great. I'm looking forward to hearing any news they might have."

Blake nodded, hands on hips, and scanning the room.

I wondered if he could hear the blood in my veins quicken with my pulse.

I pretended to look over the leather-bound ledger book I'd started keeping when I took over The Dusty Bunny. The room seemed so small, and Blake's presence was too big here. I couldn't escape him, but the worst part was I wasn't sure I wanted to, and I didn't know what to do with those feelings. Every moment we'd spent on the trail together seemed like yesterday, and yet forever ago.

When I ventured a glance in his direction, he hadn't moved. I could've sworn there was more he wanted to say, not that he'd said much, but when he didn't speak, I nodded to the door. "Get one of the girls to get you some...food?" My arm ached at the memory, and maybe my heart was a little jealous.

He nodded and smiled, and the world was a little brighter for it. He had that kind of effect. I didn't think it was only because he was a vampire either, though he'd told me vampires were more charismatic than humans. Mainly so they could lure people in to be feasted on.

I shivered.

"Yes, ma'am." He wasn't being glib. Not wholly anyway.

"Blake?" My voice cracked and I held tight to the edge of the desk.

He turned at the door to look back at me, his eyes holding the glance a moment beyond what was comfortable.

"Be gentle and don't forget to tip." Even without Donley paying him for anyone he brought through The Rift, Blake had plenty of money. He could be good to my girls.

He tipped the hat he had only just put back onto his head. "Ma'am." His voice was smooth and deep, the kind that reminded me of honey or fresh maple syrup. No matter how many times I imagined it in my head, my memory never did that sweet tone the justice it deserved.

When he walked out the door, I didn't waste but a second staring at the spot he'd just left before I ripped open Uncle Silas's letter.

CLAIRE

When I left for the day an hour later, I left Cherry—she had bright, red hair, a fitting name—in charge. She was my trusted help at the saloon because, after everything she'd been through, I trusted her. She'd been honest in the bad situation with Donley and had proven herself many times since. She wanted to help the people enslaved in The Rift as much as I did, and I trusted her completely.

I looked out over the field behind the saloon—a few houses dotted the landscape. Nobody was a small town, and I'd grown to like the sense of community.

It was amazing to have such great friends and routine. I hadn't really had that back in Boston. A few purple and blue fireflies blinked in the field next to the saloon and I watched their dance for a moment. When I'd first seen them, I didn't think I'd ever get used to them, but now they seemed as common as cheap whiskey.

I blew out a long breath and tried to release the tension in my shoulders. I'd spoken to the other Riders briefly in my office, and they'd gathered some useful information, but nothing that changed the direction of our plans. If anything, the village they'd visited was more open to collaboration than I had expected. That meant they might help us out, and we needed all the help we'd be able to wrangle. We'd marked the trip a success, even though the news hadn't been extensive.

At least the town's wards hadn't been discovered.

I headed home, which wasn't far from the bar. My new place was a not-so-small mansion Donley had owned before I relieved him of the responsibility of ownership when I took possession of the saloon. The house had ten bedrooms, an ornate oak staircase, and floors that shined like the morning sun off a clear lake. Some of the floors were marble and the kitchen floor looked like hewn limestone, though the coloring was much different than what I had seen before. Tall ceilings arched over most rooms, and every room had its own style and quirk. The front of the house was white clapboard with pillars that went from the roof overhang to the ground in front and shutters painted black at the windows.

The house reminded me of some of the houses near Boston and on the banks of the rivers outside New York City. Tall, elegant, cold, and soulless.

There were enough rooms to feel ostentatious and I had already started planning for how to make room for more girls to live with me. I didn't need the whole house to live in. Even if I had an army living in the fancy rooms—the Fae King would easily take it over and make it his own. He might take it just because of its beauty, or just because it was there. From the stories I heard, he didn't need much reason to do the terrible things he did.

The stars spotted and flickered in the dark sky, and I wondered if we'd have clear weather for a few days or if we'd have another storm like the one last week that had flooded the streets so much that the drunken Hadley brothers ended up passed out flat on their backs in mud up to their noses.

My house was close enough to the Bunny that I could walk to and from home safely, especially since the conspirators had been dealt with and crime had all but ceased to exist, at least in Nobody. I never felt ill at ease, unless the always present buzz of fear of the Fae King lurking counted for something.

I felt at home in Nobody.

Of course, neither the lack of crime, the proximity of my house, nor my ability to protect myself stopped Blake from stalking me and calling it *making sure I got home safely*. I had reminded him many times that I could take care of myself, and that I had the guns to prove it, but he still insisted on walking with me when he could.

He fell into step beside me as I walked the cobbled path between my saloon and home. The night air was cool-ish for July when I turned to him and rolled my eyes for what felt like the hundredth night in a row.

"I don't need you holding my apron strings." I purposely kept my tone droll, but I couldn't control my eyes. They raked over him, took in the details of his face, the eyes so dark brown they looked black, especially in the moonlight, the slightest hint of his smile. "I'm safe here. I don't need saving."

He nodded, not missing a footstep. "I know."

That was all he said. Like it was explanation enough. I chewed my bottom lip and stared out at the fields beyond the town. Somewhere out there, the Fae King was looking for us. Looking for me. And I was out walking the streets with an odd-stick vampire.

The slight crescent of the moon lit the path and I stepped carefully over the cobblestones that had loosened since the path had been put in. I didn't look at Blake. I didn't have to. I could feel his presence the same as if I were touching him.

Or if he were touching me.

My face heated and I turned away, pretending to look at the dog that wandered down the side street we passed.

For as much as I complained, resisted, and pretended like I didn't want him around, I enjoyed Blake's company. More so, I enjoyed that he cared enough to see me home, although that was something I was *never* going to say out loud. Uncle Silas would probably fuss at me for that one.

"How was your trip across?" I was not the best at small talk. I could hunt, shoot a bow, a rifle, a shotgun. I could bait a line, reel in a fish, clean it and cook it over a fire. Idle chatter perplexed me. Get me started on a topic I knew something about, and that was another matter. I could shoot my mouth off with the best of them. Give me cards and whiskey? I'd rival anyone in the room. But alone with Blake?

Awkward. He wasn't any better at it, either.

Did anyone enjoy the chit chat unless it served a purpose or distraction? I smoothed my skirt and folded my hands properly in front. Shoulders back, I tried to keep pace with his longer strides.

"Same as always." He swallowed and a gulp echoed in harmony with the crickets chirping. His answer didn't tell me much, like if the dangers that lurked near the crossing had come calling for him, and he'd beaten them or if by some miracle he'd been able to pass without issue.

I realized he'd never really told me much about that part of his job. Vampires were one of the few creatures that could travel both sides of The Rift without harm, but he kept most of the details secret. Most creatures couldn't return to the other side once they came to this one.

Like me. I was stuck here. All humans who came to this side were stuck here for good.

We approached my house, the parlor glowing deep gold from the light inside, and rectangles of light spilling onto the porch.

Blake walked me to the stairs at the center of the wrap around porch and paused. His body was toned, lean muscled, and tall enough I had to look up to see his smile when he walked me up the stairs to the door.

We stood for a moment longer than was comfortable and I looked away.

He cleared his throat. "Goodnight, Claire." This time his voice was husky, and the sound washed over me. He lifted his hand like he was going to brush a lock of hair from my face, but then moved away without touching me.

I almost couldn't reply but managed to swallow the lump in my throat. "Goodnight, Blake."

Like he did every night, he waited until I was inside, then he went back the way he came. I never knew where he went, but it wasn't back to the saloon. Nor did he take pleasure from any of the girls, or sustenance. They would have told me if he did. He must have had a place in town or close by—maybe a house in the woods or in the fields.

He never mentioned it.

I wasn't knowledgeable about the day to day of vampires, but even if I were, I would imagine that Blake's daily routines were different. He was a different kind of vampire than the ones I'd seen or heard about. He wasn't a monster, trying to best humans and take advantage of them. He wasn't always in search of a meal or an opportunity.

Blake seemed like a good guy. Well, except that he brought me into The Rift knowing I'd never be able to leave. A bit of anger stirred in my stomach, but it faded quickly.

He never asked to come inside my house, even under the guise of talking about the plan to save more people, or to talk about re-warding the town or any number of other business topics. Not even to talk about what happened to Donley. I didn't know what I would've said if he did, but he hadn't asked.

Before he turned to take the trail back, he circled my house, using his heightened vampire senses to make sure that there were no intruders or lurkers anywhere nearby. I'd asked him before what he was doing, and he'd told me he liked to be sure no one was waiting to attack. He did make me feel safer.

I still preferred to tend to myself, and I could do it, too. Besides, Blake Rider set me off in ways I didn't like to be set off. I had things to do that didn't involve those feelings.

I shut the door behind me and leaned against the wood for a second. My body reacted to Blake—my heart fluttered, and my stomach trembled.

Tonight, he'd even made my knees weak, and I needed to collect myself. I closed my eyes and gently touched my cheek, pretending it was Blake's touch, not my own. I ran my fingers down my neck, feeling the soft skin and soft touch of flesh against flesh.

A cold shiver raced up my spine and tingled along my flesh.

I smiled and leaned closer, then sighed. No matter. It wasn't Blake. It would never be Blake. I took another deep breath and let the thoughts and feeling sort themselves. I had work to do, and I couldn't let Blake be the reason I failed to help those in need. No matter how charming he was, I couldn't let him distract me.

Before I took my last calming breath, Neev bounced in from the sitting room. "Miss Claire! I've made you dinner."

"You did what?"

"I made dinner. Come eat."

I couldn't help but smile. "Thank you."

He'd made me dinner every night since we moved into the old Donley place two months ago. The gesture was so kind, I could've wept, but I didn't. Instead, I smiled at him again. I was tired after such a long day at the saloon, and not having to scrounge up food was such a gift. Neev was so special.

He wanted to be older. Be helpful. He was so grateful for his rescue, but it sometimes was awkward because everyone deserved a chance to be happy and the way he acted it didn't seem like he thought that was true.

No one deserved the life he had been living at that time. He'd been enslaved, with no concern for his well-being or health or life. It was terrible, and there was no way I was leaving him there.

Neev was an elf born with the ability to communicate with animals. All animals. Some other elves were blessed with the same gift, but they were either enslaved by the Fae King as Neev had been, or they were killed outright when the gift was discovered. Neev was lucky he'd been saved, or maybe I was lucky to have been able to save him.

I wasn't sure which.

His ability was one of the most special magical powers in existence, but he looked on it as the most normal thing in the world. I would have loved to have the ability.

He did sometimes call me "Claire Little Wolf", which amused me. I knew my surname meant little wolf in Old French, but I found it difficult to believe that an elf in another land would know. He said the wolves had told him, and I had no reason not to believe him. I guess I was surprised that he knew and that it was an accurate thing—even here in The Rift.

Neev was special in many ways.

"You coming?" He yawned. "Going to get cold."

I nodded. "I'm coming. I'm hungry tonight."

He giggled. "Claire Little Wolf is always hungry."

"Very funny." I put my hands on my hips. "I'm hungry on days that end in 'y'."

Neev was fifteen and itching to pay the Fae King back for the tortures he'd suffered, but he looked younger, maybe ten. Certainly not old enough to fight the Fae King with any chance of winning. And I couldn't let him get hurt. I tried to keep him out of our plans, though he often begged to be included, and I'd see him peeping around at meetings. I wanted him to enjoy his freedom, not be always looking for revenge.

"I love to cook." He grinned. "So, you're a lucky wolf tonight. There's food for you."

"I know. And I appreciate it." I wished I knew how to reach him with something besides a smile, but I didn't. Regardless, I couldn't let him go to war and fight.

Not because he cooked and cleaned for me which he certainly did, and way better than I would. Not because he cared for Peggy—the pegasus I'd rescued from the clutches of the Fae. Not because he could speak to animals or any other reason he could give.

I didn't want him fighting because he was innocent and there was a light in him that war would extinguish. He'd not had a chance to enjoy life yet, and I would never forgive myself if he died without time to enjoy his freedom. He deserved time to feel the grass under his feet and the wind on his neck and the sunshine on his cheeks without fear.

He'd seen enough pain.

By the time I was born, the Revolutionary War was long over in the United States, but I'd heard the tales of men gone crazy from the memories they couldn't outrun. I couldn't let such misery befall Neev.

"Neev. You don't have to cook for me every night. Just make food for yourself." I kept a good stock of grain and sugar, oats, ground corn and garden vegetables. He made good use of it all. "I can make food when I get home."

He grinned like we didn't have this conversation

every day. We did. "I know. But I like to cook for you. Let me cook!"

I slung an arm around his waist and hugged him. "You're too good for this world, Neev."

Maybe he'd been a slave too long. He hadn't shared much of his story with me even after all the months he'd lived with me, not more than the scant details, anyway. And I didn't push. He would tell when he could.

And I would listen.

"I like to help Little Wolf."

"Well, thank you again," I accepted defeat. I was no match for his cheery, yet firm, gently pushing. I was tired.

"After I eat, I'm going out to the barn to visit Peggy. You go on to bed and I'll clean up."

He yawned and nodded. He looked like a child, and it was hard not to treat him as one. Hard to remember he was almost a man who didn't need me mothering him.

So, I did it anyway.

Neev and I were quite peas in a pod that way.

When his door clicked shut, I quickly ate dinner then cleaned up as quietly as I could so as not to disturb him. He'd made a dinner of roasted vegetables in a light and airy pastry that rivaled the best chefs' cooking I'd ever tasted. I didn't know how he learned to cook, but he had a talent that maybe rivaled his magical ability of talking to animals. He'd not ever made a thing I didn't love.

I listened for a moment, but there was no sound in the house at all.

He was a pretty sound sleeper for an elf.

I lit a small lantern, grabbed a couple of carrots from the bin, and headed out to check on Peggy. Peggy—short for Pegasus—was a male with a wide wingspan and a coat of the blackest fur with a mane to match. He, too, had been a captive of the Fae King.

Neev had told me that Peggy was too violent to be of use to the king's army because he attacked any soldier who got within striking distance. Didn't matter that the king had apparently tried to pamper him and give him everything he could possibly want —Peggy wanted no part of helping evil.

Peggy was a good guy.

By the time we got to him, he was not much more than an enslaved creature, much like Neev. Of course we had to save him, just as we would've saved any creature the fae were preying on. I clenched the lantern handle. I couldn't tolerate when someone took advantage of someone else.

Peggy's rescue made him mine whether I wanted him or not. Fortunately, I loved him the moment I saw him and never had a pegasus been more wanted. He was free to leave if he wanted, but Neev said he liked staying with us and loved being able to help free others from the fae.

The barn was mostly dark, even with my lantern, and I paused in the doorway while my eyes adjusted. I held the lantern up to cast a strip of light into the dark barn so I could see how to get to Peggy. His stall was midway back on the right wall, with a gated top to keep him in—more for show than reality. No one here tried to make Peggy do anything.

Peggy came to the door to his stall, dipping his head and shaking his mane. I petted his nose and gave him a kiss on the warm space above it, below his eyes. He was a beautiful creature and one more time, I marveled at my luck at finding him. He sniffed my hair and give me a few licks on the head until I giggled and pushed him back.

"Peggy!" I squealed.

He was magnificent.

Sunshine snorted from her stall. Sounded like we'd woken her up.

"Shhh!" I held my finger to my lips and leaned close to Peggy.

I smiled at the memory of when he'd met Sunshine. He had done everything but prance on his back legs to get Blake's mare's attention. She wasn't having any part of it though—she probably thought he was all pretty on the outside and no substance on the inside. I'd certainly met men who fit that description.

I clicked open his stall and stepped in. Neev kept the area pristine, and Peggy had plenty of clean hay and fresh water. Peggy's stall was the largest in the barn, but he needed it because of his large wings, even though he wasn't often inside. Soft piles of golden hay covered all areas of the floor and made a cozy and safe resting place for him.

"No love for poor Peggy." I fed him a carrot to soften the blow of my words, brushed his coat under his wings, all the while murmuring to him. I didn't know if he understood although Neev said he did, but I kept talking and sometimes it seemed like he nodded in agreement.

I hoped he understood me. He had become one of the best things about being stuck this side of The

Rift. If I'd not gotten on that train, I'd never have seen a pegasus, or an elf, or a vampire. What a world had been hidden from humans.

My mother would have loved Peggy. I smiled. Uncle Silas had told me endless stories of what an amazing rider she had been and how she loved horses. What would she have thought about a winged horse? I gave Peggy another pat on the back, and he blinked at me, his long black lashes curling and framing his bright eyes. Did he miss his mother like I missed mine?

Had he lost his mother when he was young? I'd have to get Neev to ask him some day. For now, Peggy seemed happy to have me, and I was flush with love for him.

I gave him a few more brushes and pats, and more than a few more cuddles. I told him goodnight and secured his stall. Sunshine stood at her gate to watch me leave, and I offered her the other carrot. She tugged it into her stall and gave me a head bob of thanks as she munched it.

"Night, Sunshine."

I peeked in on Peggy as I passed his stall, then locked everything up and left the barn. As I headed back to the house, I searched the sky for any signs of danger, but the moon and stars seemed to blink back happiness and security. I tried to relax, but I knew that not too far away, evil was brewing and planning. I hoped the wards would hold—I didn't want Nobody to be compromised.

The house was quiet, with Neev certainly in deep sleep by now. Even after I washed up and set my clothing out to freshen up for morning and crawled into my bed, I wasn't tired. Well, perhaps my body was, but my mind wasn't. Instead, it was busy longing, yearning even, for Blake.

We'd shared a moment, one of the most intimate in my life. The most erotic. I didn't know that feeding a vampire could be so arousing. I hadn't even known about vampires being real till I met him, but now it seemed the most natural thing in the world.

Even though he was a vampire, he was also all man, all power and strength. The touch of his hand on my arm, the strong grip...I was too...excited to sleep. Too wound up over a man who lied to me, tried to trick me, was going to deliver me to Donley without a second thought.

Still, I wanted him.

It made no sense.

I'd wanted to... heat burned inside of me as I thought of all the things I'd wanted to do to him as he fed. All the things I wanted his soft lips to do to my skin.

I would never forget how they felt as they slipped and brushed against my sensitive skin. He was warm and soft and breathless.

Rhythmic.

But these thoughts were my escape, the ones I only allowed myself when he wasn't around, when I couldn't still smell the enticing scent of him.

My room was warm, warmer than I liked, and I went to the window and threw open the sash and breathed in the night air. I lit the lantern and moved it to the sill, perching it on the thin strip of wood and letting the light spill out into the darkness. A gentle breeze made the flame flicker and dance, but I was still wrapped in the memory of Blake touching me.

I didn't want to be.

I wanted to forget the whole thing because it would make working with him and sending him out to gather information less nerve-racking. We had a job to do, and these feelings could jeopardize everything. All the work, all the plans, all the people. We could lose even more if I let my feelings take over.

If I let how I *felt* take over.

But I hadn't experienced these feelings before,

and I wanted more, even though every bit of my brain screamed more.

When I moved away from the window, I left it open. The night air helped me sleep and tonight I was going to need all the help I could get.

I slid beneath the cool sheets and tried not to think of him, tried to not imagine his hands and his mouth and, oh, his smile. But I failed. The dreams came, setting me to tremble in the night, alone.

What dreams they were.

3

BLAKE

I made a last round of her house, listening, smelling, watching. No one jumped from the shadows, and nothing happened that required I stick around for her protection, even though there was a part of me that wanted to stick around.

Stick around...for a long time.

The corruption that used to exist in Nobody seemed to have been weeded out over the last couple months, but there were still plenty of men here who didn't particularly like Claire or the fact that she was more man than some of them. Some didn't like the fact that she waltzed in and took the saloon and they continued to challenge her. Most were probably glad she ousted Donley, but they weren't going to admit that. They didn't like giving credit where it was due.

Claire was a surprise. She could out drink, out play, out ride all the men I knew in the territory. She seemed to enjoy besting anyone who challenged her, and it didn't bother her to wake snakes no matter who came hunting for a ruckus.

I gave the area one more onceover and headed to the barn to get Sunshine. The day had been long enough that even though I didn't need as much rest as a human, I was wearing a bit thin. The barn door was latched up and I flipped it open and went in.

The pegasus snorted when he heard me, and Sunshine nickered in reply. I didn't know the language they were speaking, but it seemed to me that she wasn't impressed with his noise. I laughed. Didn't we all have the same problems. I gave him a nod as I passed his stall then I got Sunshine out and moved to the tack table to get her dressed.

Once she was saddled, I rode her out of the barn and into the night. I could have found my way home whether there was moon or not, but tonight there was moon a plenty. Sunshine clip-clopped, happy to be taking an easy stroll and I leaned into thinking about the time ahead of us when we'd be facing the fae. How many people would we lose?

How many more would we save? Would we be doing anything if Claire hadn't come to help us organize?

The questions weighed on my mind. Claire had already shown us that we have to move on the evil in the land before it takes over. We can't wait and just hope it doesn't affect us.

I rode the dusty trail between on my way home, but before I turned at the halfway bend, Aaron— another vampire and rider I'd sent out to find Clayton—waved me to a stop.

I sensed his frantic energy before we were close, and I settled Sunshine into a stop until we could be sure that the vampire wasn't turning on us.

"Blake," he gave a nod.

Aaron was a Drakeborne vampire, which meant he had potential to be one of the greatest Riders on the trail and possibly the greatest vampire ever. Genetics made him faster, stronger, and possessing enhanced senses compared to other vampires.

Even compared to me, and I was well ahead of most vampires.

"What is it, Aaron? Is everything okay?" I nudged Sunshine to settle into a stop beside Aaron.

"We have Clayton cornered outside of town in the old Clemson shack."

"By the lake?" I asked. That was an odd place for him to be.

"Yes."

Aaron was part of the group of Riders I'd sent to find Clayton. Once upon a time Clayton had been a Rider with the Pony Express on this side of The Rift. He delivered the letters from the vampires and fae and shifters on this side of The Rift to humans on the other and vice versa. But then he went rogue. Sold himself to the Fae King and his services to anyone else who was willing to pay for whatever unsavory job that needed to be done.

I drew in a sharp breath. We needed Clayton.

Clayton knew what the Fae King had planned, and we *needed* to know too. So, he was valuable to us, more so alive, even though I wanted him dead. If Aaron and the others had him locked down, I needed to be there. I knew how to get to the shack, so I didn't wait for him to follow.

Sunshine sliced through the night air, her hoofbeats pounding against the dirt as she raced toward the shack at the water's edge. The weather was cooperating in so much as the lake hadn't flooded in the recent rain so the small road to the cabin which truly was more of a shack was passable.

Although, with Sunshine, most roads were. She

was strong. Tough. Battle trained. Smart. This horse knew when to hold back and when to charge ahead. The fact that she slowed on her own now, meant she sensed danger.

The first shot zinged past, and I felt the wind of it as it nearly scraped my face. It would drop soon, hopefully before it came near Aaron who'd fallen back as I raced to the edge of the lake. I scanned the area as quickly as I could, but I wasn't as quick as I needed to be to avoid trouble. I didn't see anyone nearby, but the cabin and woods provided plenty of room for someone to hide. The hair on my arms stood on end in warning, but I had no time to react.

The second shot whistled through the air and pierced the skin over my right shoulder, sending a bolt of scalding heat through me. I must have yelped, though I didn't hear myself make a sound as my vision went white with pain. Sunshine startled under me, but I held her steady with a tight grip of my knees. The force of the hit left me shaking and weak, but I knew I had to move or be at risk of getting hit again. I leaned forward on Sunshine, gripping the reins with my good hand.

The wound would heal quickly, but the next few minutes would be extremely inconvenient and painful. I couldn't draw my gun with only one hand to guide Sunshine. The other arm dangled uselessly at my side with my bone broken where my arm connected to my shoulder.

The pain jolted through me with every step Sunshine took, with every canter of her hooves as she moved. We were in the open now, and she could go a bit faster. Maybe we'd escape being hit again. A horse blew past me, his rider pale, his skin mottled and greyish.

Clayton.

He'd escaped, which didn't say much for the ability of the Riders to hold him. Of course they couldn't. It was Clayton. The rogue vampire. Smart one, too.

Damn it!

I should have known it was too good to be true that we'd caught him and could hold him for any length of time. No, he wasn't going to make it easy.

I turned Sunshine in the direction he fled, the bone in my shoulder already mending around the bullet, although my arm was still not functional. Stiffness replaced the burning pain, and I could see shapes well again instead of blotches. I urged Sunshine on, pushing her to try to catch the horse ahead of us on the trail. From the sounds of hooves trampling the ground, I knew that others followed us, but I was more aware of trying to maintain my balance while keeping Sunshine on the path through the trees.

We had the best chance of catching Clayton, and that wasn't saying much. Somehow, he was getting farther from us with every second that passed.

Sunshine zigged and zagged around lower tree branches, chasing the horse in front of her while other Riders fell in behind. We passed the edge of the lake and started up the mountain trail through the thick woods and tall grasses, every step steeper than the last. Hoofbeats echoed off scattered rock faces, and sounds seemed to come from all directions. With the faint moonlight playing tricks on the shimmering rocks and casting wriggling shadows in every direction, I couldn't be sure of which way we were going, other than the fact Sunshine heaved with the strain of going up, up, up.

We rounded a long bend in the trail, and suddenly I couldn't see Clayton anymore, or his horse. The top of the mountain blocked the moon's light from this side, and my eyes stained against the darkness. I couldn't tell the sound of Clayton's horse from any one of ours.

I slowed Sunshine to a trot, and peered into the

woods, trying to see any hint of where Clayton might have gone.

Nothing.

There was no point in continuing. We'd lost him. I whistled for Aaron. When he replied, I shouted, "We lost him. Search is over. Let's get back to the valley."

Damn. Clayton may have won this round, but I wasn't giving up. I'd never give up. There would be time to catch him, and I would catch him. I had to believe so.

The others headed down the trail in front of me, but I sat still for a moment, listening to the quietening landscape. I didn't want to give up. Sunshine breathed heavily from the strain of the chase but stood still as she awaited my next direction. An owl hooted in the distance, and another returned the call from deep in the forest. I couldn't scent them, so they were far away. No sign of Clayton at all, either. He'd simply disappeared.

I curled my hand into a fist and gritted my teeth, fighting the urge to yell. He was a key figure in our plans.

That he'd escaped wasn't news that would make Claire happy, but she had to be told. We'd been hoping to use him to fill in the gaps in the Fae King's plans, but it was an unlikely outcome anyway. We'd get him.

One way or another.

I eased Sunshine down the mountain to meet up with the other Riders. They waited by a copse of oak trees near the lake. Aaron sat on his horse, a gray mare that was amazingly muscled. She turned toward us as I guided Sunshine near them.

"We have to let the other towns know that Clayton's a traitor before he causes serious trouble." I tugged at the reins to keep Sunshine in check. She wasn't a fan of other horses getting too close and Aaron's mare was snipping at her.

"What about Miss Claire?" Aaron sat up straight on his horse. "She needs to be told he got away."

I considered him for a long minute, even as the tendrils of his power floated out around him like long strands of silken cord. He was attracted to her, probably had designs on her himself, but no matter what he wanted, the feeling in my belly wasn't jealousy. It was truth. The truth was Aaron Drakeborne could just damned well stay away from *Miss Claire*.

As could the rest of them.

"I'll deliver the message myself." I stared him straight in the eyes. "You don't need to worry about her."

He nodded, nose in the air. No matter how strong he was, or how revered, he knew when he was overstepping. "Very well. What's next? What do you need?"

I scanned the scene. Riders milled about, some on horseback, and others leading their horses around. We were lucky to have such a crew to help us. With so many good witches on our side, and others who believed in the cause, we might stand a chance against the fae. The wards would protect Nobody, as long as we kept up with the positioning. The markers had only just been moved, but I would stress the need to move them again tomorrow.

Better safe than regretful. With Clayton lose, we couldn't be sure if he had the means to reveal our position.

I turned to Aaron. "You go to Amberhill and make sure they know that there's a bounty on taking Clayton alive. Make it a big one—we've got the coin to put behind it. Make sure they know he's a traitor, too, and use the network to spread the word among the settlements."

"We'll get it done. That no-good piece-of-dirt vampire is going to get his due. Sooner or later, he'll answer to me."

"We need to get what we need from him first."

"We will. I promise you that. We're going to close the net on him before he can whimper to the fae." Aaron pivoted his horse to face the other Riders as he spoke to me. "We'll return as soon as we can."

Before I could answer, he was putting the plan into action. He took two of his men, set them on different paths to Amberhill and sent the rest back to wherever they came from or to other spots. I couldn't hear all his directions—I just knew he was in command, and they were listening.

I appreciated his diligence, and his desire to make sure if he or one of his men didn't make it to Amberhill or was captured, there would be someone left to deliver the message. Clayton stood a good chance of being caught.

There weren't many men I trusted, but Aaron Drakeborne was one vampire I did trust with most everything.

As the men dispersed, I dismounted and led Sunshine down to the lake shore to get a sip of water. She'd done well on the chase and a few minutes of rest would be great for both of us. We'd head home soon and try to relax before morning and telling Claire about what happened.

The crescent moon mirrored itself in the still lake and Sunshine sent tiny ripples across the glassine surface as she lapped. I kept an easy lookout but marveled at the mountains reflecting in the lake and the way they looked like teeth in a giant mouth. Seemed like danger lurked everywhere. Maybe once the fae were defeated, things would calm down some.

I splashed water on my face and wiped the wetness off on my sleeve. The cool night air tingled and sent a shiver down my back.

My night had been full and there wasn't much left for me to do but go home. I was sure that Sunshine would agree. She would want to sleep late too, and maybe have an extra ration of hay and maybe a couple of carrots for her efforts.

I stuck my hands in my pockets and stared across the dark lake.

I had to tell Claire about Clayton's escape, but I knew it wasn't critical enough to wake her up in the middle of the night—she needed her rest what with running the saloon full time. She'd be up in a couple hours to get to work. It could wait.

Besides, Clayton would most likely still be running free tomorrow.

CLAIRE

By morning, I'd had more than one steamy dream, and Blake had been front and center in each. I wanted to be annoyed, to think that it was ridiculous for him to be taking up so much of my sleeping time and to somehow make it his fault, but even I couldn't figure out how he could possibly be to blame. So, I pretended like I hadn't spent a night kissing him and making love with him in my mind while I slept.

What else would a proper lady do? It wasn't like I had asked to dream about him.

Besides, ladies didn't speak of such things aloud. While I wasn't much of a lady in some respects, I didn't talk about things of that nature either.

Instead, I went to the kitchen and made myself eggs and bacon over the wood stove then sat down to eat. Neev wasn't up yet or if he was, he'd already beat me to the barn to care for Peggy. Not that Peggy was high maintenance. He wasn't, but he liked to be brushed morning and night. Afternoon too if he could get it.

He was a vain pegasus, truth be told. Praising his beauty while brushing him? He liked that even more.

The coffee was still hot when I touched the pot and so Neev had to be outside. Coffee didn't warm itself. I closed my eyes and inhaled the deep and hearty aroma. "Ahhh." There wasn't anything in the world like it. I hadn't been much of a coffee drinker before arriving in The Rift, but I'd adopted a pretty big habit since, given my long hours at the saloon. Some coffee here was brought through The Rift from the other side, and it was especially flavorful and in demand here. Apparently, it was in short supply back home because of the Civil War and supplies there, so it was even more difficult to obtain here. Fortunately, Donley had a robust supply laid up already, so when I took over, I gained access to that supply.

With the kitchen fires already alight, Neev

could've been up for hours already, but I hadn't heard a sound.

I poured coffee into a mug from the cupboard then sat and ate quietly, not thinking of Blake. Not on purpose anyway, but one thought always led to another which somehow managed to bring me back to thinking about him as I sipped the rich brew. I didn't understand the connections between thought and memory sometimes, and other times I couldn't trace the path backward to the start, but every turn brought me around to Blake.

Why couldn't I get that man, that *vampire*, out of my thoughts? Had coming to The Rift made me weak of mind? I didn't think so. If anything, I felt stronger and more independent. Blake was an unusual and unwelcome interruption to my thoughts.

As I shoved another bite through my teeth, I chewed thoughtfully and a picture of him flittered into my mind. He *was* a beautiful man. Although not the first I'd ever seen. Only the first I wasn't about to stop thinking about. Part of the difference was that he wasn't just handsome on the outside. He was smart and thoughtful and mannerly too. He was...different.

He was also annoying.

I turned my cup up and finished the coffee. I didn't have any more time to spend on Blake Rider. I had work to do.

I left the coffee pot on the stove and carried my dishes to the stove where I stuck them in the cleaning pail and gave them a good scrub and rinse in the water pail before setting them out to dry before they could be returned to the cupboard. I wouldn't give Neev more to do, or rather, more he felt he *had* to do. He did more than enough already.

I dried my hands and headed to the barn to check on Peggy. The morning dew hadn't dried yet and cast a net of rainbows across the grass. Birdsong filled the air, and it seemed every local animal was out enjoying the morning before the heat of the day became oppressive. Neev wasn't at the barn either, so I started brushing Peggy myself.

He stomped his hoof in approval. He was bristling with energy and excitement like he wanted to go out for a run or a flight around Nobody. Maybe I'd have time later, or maybe Neev could take him out later.

"Oh, pretty Peggy. You wouldn't believe the week we've had round here." As I brushed, I filled my pegasus in on the happenings at the saloon. I told Peggy things I didn't tell anyone else. Neev could understand the animals and they understood him, so I assumed whether or not Peggy could communicate with me, he understood when I spoke to him.

I'd told him all about Blake one night after I'd had a few too many at the bar. I'd also fallen asleep in his stall and awakened in the morning shielded by his soft, dark wing. I'd told him how much I missed Uncle Silas and how there were times I wished I'd never seen that ad for a mail-order bride.

I didn't know if I meant that part or not, seeing as it had turned out that coming to live in Nobody had made quite a difference in my life—though I didn't yet know if that was good or bad, overall. Most days, I liked being in Nobody, where I could handle most of my own business and not have so many constraints on me just because I was a woman. I had power to make my own choices about so many things, with not a lot of pushback just because of being female.

That was a great thing.

But I really did miss Uncle Silas.

It wasn't fair that I had to choose.

I forced the impending tears back. No time to cry, even though Uncle Silas had taught me that tears weren't a weakness—they were a strength. Anyone who wasn't afraid to cry in front of others was brave. They were comfortable showing emotion. Comfortable in who they were.

Peggy stared at me as I brushed the coat under his mane on his neck, where a few small tangles made him jerk back at the snags. "I know, big guy. This is a tough time, or I would let you out to fly whenever you want."

He nodded his head then nuzzled my shoulder.

"I know. You would always come back." I smiled at him and ran my fingers through his mane, letting it fall like water over my hand. I turned and twisted my wrist like I'd never seen anything like his beautiful mane before. But really, it was true. He gleamed and sparkled like something magical. Almost like the rainbow of dew I'd seen on the grass earlier—but more fluid. Like a waterfall in slow motion. Maybe a waterfall of black silk with rainbow strands...

I sighed. I loved my Peggy so much. I kissed him on the forehead.

"You know, Peggy..." He used to bristle when I called him that or snort, but these days, he just dealt with it. Or I assumed so, anyway. "I know what the Fae King did to you. And his plan. What he was going to do to me. Again, his plan." Peggy nodded again like he was encouraging me to go on. "I want to free all his hostages. What he does to humans and to elves and pegasus is... criminal. It's evil, and I can't let him get away with it."

Peggy nodded and bared his teeth in a horsey smile.

"He agrees with you." Neev opened the gate and came into the stall. "He hates the Fae King as much as I do."

"Neev..." I turned to see the elf. "Good morning. You startled me."

"Sorry." He looked at the ground and kicked at the hay. "If not for you, he would've been killed." Quieter, Neev added, "We both would be dead."

My heart ached to hug Neev and Peggy and never let them go. "Even if I didn't know how it was going to turn out, I would do the same things all over again." And I meant that. I could've never walked away from either of them. And I never would. They were my family now.

"I never knew freedom until I came to live here." He smiled. "With you."

"In some ways, I didn't know true freedom either." I brushed Peggy's neck. "Nothing like what you've been through, but women in my world don't have the freedoms that men do."

"I've heard. Some of that is true here, too."

I kept brushing. "Yes, that's true. But we will

keep up the good fight to make sure everyone is free from oppression."

"You're amazing, Claire Little Wolf."

I heard the smile in his voice, but I didn't turn to look. "Thank you, Neev." I brushed a few more strokes. "I've been meaning to ask. How much do you think Peggy understands of what I say? And do you understand what he says? Is it word-for-word, or more just the general idea?"

I made sure not to look at Neev. He was always so nervous to talk about himself and I didn't want to make him feel anxious. But I really wanted to know if Peggy understood me. It could make all the difference in battle.

"Well," Neev began. "I can understand animals, that's true." He paused.

"I thought all elves could." To be honest, until I met Neev, I hadn't known much of anything. Not that vampires existed, or shifters, elves, fae, and certainly a pegasus was only in stories. But here I was. Across a rift no humans knew existed. None I knew anyway.

Neev shook his head. "Most can understand at least generally. But when this king came to power, those who could understand clearly what was being spoken had to start hiding because he had his men taking us away from our families. One by one, we were taken and made slaves for him. We were killed if we refused to cooperate."

I paused brushing and looked at Neev. He was so small still. He must have been a small child when he was taken. The horror of what he had endured was just beginning to be revealed, and it was dark. My heart hurt for him, and I didn't want to push him to share anything that made him uncomfortable.

"That's horrible." I didn't know what else to say.

He nodded. "I lost many friends" He laid his hand on Peggy's back and looked up at me. "You saved me. Thank you."

"We're going to save the others. All of them. I promise."

I was glad he'd told me what happened, filled me in on a bit of his life and what he'd endured. It wasn't a full story, just a piece of it. Probably the only part he felt safe to tell, but it was enough to make me sad for him. Sad for all of them. I wanted to help the elves and the women and the creatures.

This king had to be stopped. I already knew it, but every hour that passed made me surer and firmer in my conviction.

I was going to stop him.

As I continued brushing Peggy and thinking,

Neev stood with his back against the stall wall, his head down. Neither of us spoke. We'd said so much already. Shared so much. Even Peggy was quiet.

Bonded.

When Blake walked into the barn, I looked up, but only for a second. It was always that first look at him that got me. His rugged handsomeness was startling.

Intense.

I swallowed hard, and my pulse quickened.

"Claire." His voice was low and quiet. "I need a minute to speak to you in private." Every word he said was deliberate, had meaning I was too flustered to try to decipher.

It felt petty to put him off, but I was still reeling from all those dreams about him that I hadn't wanted to have.

"You'll have to wait. I'm busy." Neev would take over with the brush if I asked, but the point was, I wasn't going to ask. Not right this moment. I turned my back on Blake, hiding a small smile I couldn't control.

5

CLAIRE

I left Blake dangling for a few minutes while I brushed Peggy's back with long languid strokes.

I handed the brush to Neev and smiled. "Would you mind?"

He smiled back because of course he didn't mind. He would never mind no matter what I asked him to do. Neev was of the rare elven breed who loved doing things for others.

I dusted my hands and washed them off in the pail of water Neev had brought back from the creek. We always kept two pails of water inside the front entrance to the barn. One for drinking and one for washing hands or faces.

When I walked out of the barn, Blake was beside me, matching his step to mine though he had a much longer gait and I walked slower when I had nowhere to go, and I wanted to spend more time with him. Even though I wasn't about to admit it to anyone.

Under an old oak at the edge of the yard where the green grass met the mossy floor of the woods, I stopped and turned to Blake. He hadn't stopped as short as I hoped, or maybe he stopped just where I subconsciously planned, but he was close enough I could see the flecks of amber in his deep brown eyes.

"You wanted to speak to me. Is there a situation?" Lately, there always was. And it never seemed to be a good thing. Maybe not catastrophic, but usually a setback of some sort.

He nodded but didn't meet my gaze. I wasn't surprised particularly, but I braced myself because whatever he was about to say, I wasn't going to like it. It didn't take a genius to know it.

He blew out a long breath. "Clayton got away last night."

He told me about the chase, about the hunt up the mountain, about Clayton disappearing in the blackness of night, seemingly into the darkness without a trace. Everyone had looked for him nigh and far, and no sign of him was to be seen anywhere.

Everyone had been on edge, knowing that he was free.

I sighed because there was nothing to be done. No recrimination would bring Clayton back, and it didn't sound like anyone had been lax—Clayton had just outsmarted everyone. But knowing he was out there, a traitor to the settlements, one of the king's men, meant danger for everyone.

Clayton knew me. Knew Blake. Was as much a tracker as a Rider.

"Shit." It wasn't often I swore in front of others, but this was a situation that called for it. If not, I would excuse it anyway. "I'm going to have to move up the plans I made."

"I sent Aaron and his men to warn everyone at Amberhill and to get word of a reward out there for his capture." Blake crossed his arms and stared out over the fields. "I'm upset he got out on my watch. I feel like it's my fault."

"You weren't even there. How could it be your fault?" I shook my head. If the sun was a minute late coming up, Blake would take the blame for that too. "It's a setback, but we can overcome it. We always do. And hopefully Aaron and his men can get a lead on him in the nearby towns."

"Hopefully." Blake's mouth set in a hard line. "We've got to find him."

"We will. I'm going to get a letter ready. Can you carry it?"

"Of course."

"I'll get it ready."

I stepped around him, laid my hand on his arm for just a second, just long enough to satisfy my need to touch him, also because the effect on him was visual and I wanted to see him blink, swallow hard. It might've been wrong, might've been selfish or even vain, but I liked knowing he wasn't immune.

As I walked across the back lawn, I thought of the plan and what I would have to do to prepare. I went into the quiet house, up the stairs to my room and closed the door, leaned against it until I could get my heart and my breath under control again. Blake affected me more than I wanted to admit, but this reaction wasn't solely about him. This was about Clayton, too, about the Fae King, about the things I wished I could change.

I sat at the desk and penned a letter to my uncle.

Dear Uncle Silas:

I hope this letter finds you well, as I am. Regrettably, I must travel from my home and so this will be the last letter I send for a while and will be unable to send word. I will write you again once I return from my trip. Please, do not worry and know that I will be thinking of you while I'm away.

Yours truly,

Claire

I ran back downstairs to catch Blake. I needed him to deliver the letter to the Pony Express outpost near The Rift with as much haste as he could. He was sitting in a rocker on my porch, staring ahead and lost in thought.

"Blake?"

He looked up.

"Can you take this letter to the drop off point on the other side? Quickly?" I held the letter out. "As soon as you return, we'll make travel arrangements and plans for the next steps."

I was purposefully vague because the plan in my mind wasn't firm yet. There were details to be worked out, things that would have to happen. And I wasn't entirely sure about all of it.

Blake stared at me, and I couldn't read the expression on his face. It wasn't blankness, and it wasn't anger or fear or anything I'd ever seen before. He took the letter and paused before speaking, as if considering what he was about to say, then reconsidering. "I'll post it today." He nodded at the letter in his hand then at me. "Be safe. I'll be back as soon as I can."

The concern in his voice was like a caress against my skin and I smiled. "I'll be at the saloon, surrounded by my girls. I'll be safe there." To prove my point or at least to emphasize it, I patted the six-shooters holstered on each of my hips. "I'm quite capable of protecting myself." The fact that he cared enough to say it made me warmer, as if I'd stoked a fire in the stove and the heat had poured over me.

"I know, but you're important..." He paused as looked at me hard, like he was trying to see my heart pumping inside my chest or my mind working inside my head. "You're important to this town and to the people. Can't let anything happen to you."

My stomach fluttered and I ignored it as much as a woman could ignore a sensation like that. Instead, I walked him down the steps to where he'd tied his horse to a post out front.

"Ride swiftly but do take care." It was as personal as I could get right now with so much on my mind. This wasn't the time for an examination of feelings or anything other than keeping to the plan.

When he was gone, I used the irons heated on the stove to put the curls in my hair and then pinned the locks up, leaving some long tendrils hanging around the sides. One of the girls at the saloon had showed me how to care for the fancy up-do, and which pomades and powders to get from the coiffeur to help everything stay in place. I could now fix my hair so that I looked like one of the girls instead of like someone who was ready to head out to kill rabbits with her teeth.

Things were much different, even in Boston, where hair didn't need to withstand such harsh treatment or look fancy in the same way. Fancy hair was much tamer back east.

When my hair was up and tight enough not to fall before I came home and removed the pins, I added some rouge to my cheeks and lips, checked my reflection in the mirror, and satisfied I wouldn't scare the customers away, set off for the Bunny. I had a long day in front of me and I'd already had what felt like a full day of excitement.

I could leave the saloon in the capable hands of my ladies, but there was a lot of work to be done behind the scenes before I could leave. I didn't know how soon Blake would be back from dropping the letter, so every detail had to be taken care of now.

Just in case we needed to leave quickly.

Time was most certainly short.

6

BLAKE

Claire made me feel like I'd never been with a woman before, like I was an inexperienced boy rather than someone who'd lived two lifetimes already. I was almost to The Rift, and I was still out of sorts. From one slight touch of her hand on my arm.

On. My. Arm.

Claire was a woman. I was a man. Not a human man anymore, but did it matter in the grand scheme? I thought not. Although, right now, I wasn't asking Claire. Not while she had so many other things on her mind. She could rile me up with a word or a touch and shut me down with a look or a sigh.

No one had ever had such an ability to affect me.

I barely noticed the trail. We'd made good time, but I couldn't tell you anything different about the trip. It had been one cloud of thought and frustration.

Sunshine had made this trip about a thousand times now, and she knew the way which let me concentrate less on the trail and more on the woman whose image floated in and out across my mind at random times during the day.

I could perfectly see her long blonde hair, the green gray of her eyes, her smile. Her eyes seemed to change color depending on her mood—if she was mad, they ranged deep green and dark gray like a stormy sea. Early in the morning when she was brushing the pegasus, they were the color of bright clover.

Her smile.

Radiant wasn't even a close word to capture it—it was like a punch in the stomach. I would take that punch a thousand times a day if I could, as long as I got to see it. Her smile was the reward I didn't even know I had been looking for and yet once I saw it, I knew I'd never get enough of it.

Maddening.

I tugged at Sunshine's reins and slowed her a bit.

We were close and I needed to pay close attention to the area near the border to make sure there were no obstacles in the path. The fae wanted to be able to cross over to the human world but were unable to, so they stalked the areas they knew were crossings, hoping to capture a vampire or someone who was making the crossing.

Even though it was dark, I didn't need my vampire sight to keep to the path. Sunshine and I were in sync and soon enough, we were at the outpost across The Rift with no sign of trouble. I looped Sunshine up at the trough at the hitching post and she immediately went for the fresh water. With one more look around, I headed toward the mail outpost.

I'd mailed many a letter for Claire so the clerk—Thomas John Pierson—nodded at me as soon as I walked into the building. He was always nice to me, though his appearance could be intimidating to some, it helped him do his job. He was tall—over seven feet—and muscular. He looked like he could heft a large rock or person or both at the same time. He likely could. Point was, no one questioned him.

Today, he stood behind a wooden counter stuffing a large bag with letters and a few small parcels. The bag would go to one of the Riders for delivery to the various nearby destinations—other towns, other outposts. The operation had grown fairly large in the time I'd known about it, and was connecting more towns with every passing week.

"Hello, Blake. You have another letter for Mr. Lowell? We have a Rider leaving soon."

That was fortunate. I didn't know when another Rider would be heading that way. I wasn't sure what the procedures were anymore since the Civil War was going on.

I handed over the envelope with Claire's smooth handwriting across the front. "Claire likes to keep in touch with her Uncle Silas."

Thomas tucked the letter straight into the bag. "Silas Lowell. Good man. Or so I hear tell."

In my periphery, something moved, and I looked over at a second person in the place, probably one of the Riders or another clerk. He perked his head up at the mention of Silas's name. Maybe he knew him. Maybe he'd had dealings with him, or maybe I imagined it. Because when I looked at the man more head on, he ignored me altogether.

I nodded to Thomas, then waved over my shoulder and left.

Maybe because I hadn't eaten in a while or because I was in a hurry to get back to Claire, but I was eager to be on my way. I hadn't truly fed since I drank Claire's blood, and now that I knew what she tasted like, everything else paled in comparison. I'd had crude snacks and bits here and there—enough to survive. But it was the difference between having a home cooked meal versus trail rations. The difference between daylight in The Rift and night beyond it.

She was a perfect woman. I could see it. Even if she infuriated me and made me want her all at the same time. I couldn't escape the thoughts either. She was always right at the edge of my mind, ready to bulldoze her way in or patiently waiting until I could give her the proper consideration she deserved. But always there. And I'd never felt so... enthralled by a woman before.

I wanted to get back to her. More than wanted, if I was honest. But I didn't want to be honest. All I knew at the moment was I didn't want to be so far away from her.

It was thoughts of her that fogged my thoughts. Thoughts of her that made me lose focus, not pay attention to the Rider who'd been flaming me for the last twenty minutes. I was almost to The Rift when he overtook me.

He pulled his horse in front of Sunshine, the

dust from his quick stop billowing up and obscuring his horse's lower half. I pulled Sunshine to a halt.

He aimed his pistol at my head. I could have climbed down and disarmed him before he could blink, but this was a familiar human, someone whose scent I recognized. I wanted to see how this played out. I sniffed again, trying to figure it out.

"I don't have any money on me." I said it because he had a gun pointed at me, his hat tipped down to shadow his face. But the scent was...

"I'm not after your money." He had an accent, but I couldn't place it. I looked at him and he tilted his hat up. "You're either going to take me to my niece, Claire, or I'm going to put a bullet between your eyes and find someone else who will."

"What?"

He cocked his pistol, keeping it pointed at my head. "Was I not clear? Take me to Claire. Now."

I could take him through The Rift, but he'd never be able to come back. That was a lot of responsibility to lay on my shoulders. But he had a gun and he wanted to do it. What choice did I have?

"If I take you, you won't be able to come back." I leveled my voice, trying to be as monotone as possible.

"Bullshit, son." He scowled. "I don't believe that.

And even if it's true, I don't want to be away from my family any longer. Take me to her. Are you gonna do it or am I going to have to find someone else who will?" He steadied the gun.

I ignored my conscience and nodded. "Fine. I'll take you to her."

She will probably hate me for it.

Well, shit.

He lowered the gun and holstered it.

"Let's go, then. Time's a wasting. Name's Silas, but I think you know that. Who are you, and how did you come to know my niece?"

CLAIRE

I sat at the bar sipping a drink and pretending to do paperwork. My stomach was in knots. Every conversation around me felt like a cloud of buzzing flies swarming to bite me. It was almost all I could do to not scream.

It had been almost three days since Blake left for the human world to mail the letter to Uncle Silas. That was what I called the place I'd come from now—even though this world had humans too. That world wasn't home anymore. As much as I hated to admit it, this was home. This was the place I belonged. Although maybe I'd only decided I belonged here because I couldn't leave. It was hard to tell.

On a normal night, Blake would've been beside me at the bar, watching things unfurl the way the nights here did. I touched the seat beside me. It was cold.

On a normal night, he would smile at me, and I would pretend not to notice. I would pretend not to care.

But I always noticed, and I always cared.

Thinking about it that way, it sounded like we were courting. But we weren't. It was the way we interacted.

I missed him. Not that I was about to admit it aloud. I needed to keep what I felt for him separate from the anger I should've felt for being stuck here in this crazy beautiful land, and for his part in trapping me here.

I turned my drink up, finished it, and slammed the empty glass on the bar.

But I'd already forgiven Blake. I forgave him again every day when I thought of Uncle Silas. When I remembered the promises that were made to me by Donley acting as Raymond Buchanan, the man I'd thought I was writing back and forth with when I decided to make the trip west.

I couldn't believe how naïve I was to think it was

a good idea to answer a newspaper advertisement to become a bride. How could I think that would end up well? Even though I needed the money to help Uncle Silas, what made me think things would be so simple? I didn't know enough to realize how south things could go.

I'd learned so much in a short time. About life and about people's intentions. Things that couldn't be learned in books. Couldn't be taught but had to be experienced firsthand. Some people were out for themselves and didn't care a lick about others. Mr. Donley was one of those. He'd just as well step on someone as get his shoes dirty.

And that's partly what bothered me so much now. Blake was out traveling the trails in this crazy land. Alone. Sure, he was a vampire and had super healing and lots of other things that would help him. There were so many Donleys out there waiting to take advantage of him. Especially in this world ruled by a king who was the worst of the worst.

A group of men at one of the poker tables barked laughter and one threw his cards in the air in mock anger. I watched them for any sign of trouble, but it looked like they were having good fun. Too bad there wasn't more of that in the world.

As for Blake, I was worried about him. I

thought he was unkillable, but what if I was wrong? What if there was one bigger vampire or other creature, or stronger, faster creature than Blake? He would put up a fight, probably a good one, but what if he couldn't? What if the fight was more than he could handle? I had no idea what else this world held.

Besides, if all vampires lived forever, wouldn't the world be overrun by them by now?

I was definitely scared of the unknown and I had learned the hard way that it was a valid fear. Especially on this side of The Rift. Maybe it was more obvious here because I did remember Uncle Silas always talking about people taking advantage of others back in Boston. I was pretty sure he was talking about the hidden dangers people carried.

Life had seemed so simple.

The saloon was busy, with more customers than usual. Plenty of men gathered to drink and talk and play cards. Music tinkled from the piano while SarahBeth danced on the stage at the backside of the room, underneath the balcony that led to the rooms upstairs. She had a new act that combined pratfalls and some type of dancing she called operatic, which didn't look like anything I'd ever seen before, but customers apparently liked. People laughed and clapped and kept buying drinks, so who was I to complain?

I looked at my papers and realized I'd not been doing the math and checks I was supposed to do but drawing flowers of varying sizes across the margins. I folded the paper and handed it to Cherry.

"Please put this on my desk."

"Of course, sweetheart." She blew me a kiss and disappeared down the hallway to my office.

I waved off another drink—the last thing I needed in this mood—and resigned myself to another long night waiting on time to go home and another restless sleep while waiting on Blake to return.

I despised being so tied to my emotions that I was incapacitated.

The saloon door swung open and a gush of air—relief—whooshed out of my lungs. I wanted to call it back, because I wasn't entirely sure I appreciated the thought behind it. But then I decided to just feel what I felt.

Blake had come back, walked through the saloon door like he hadn't just kept me worried for three days. Suddenly, the worry was gone. Completely.

I was thankful he'd come back. Grateful for his return and the days away didn't matter so much anymore. How was it possible that all that emotion could just evaporate like that in an instant?

I wasn't a woman who displayed a lot of emotion. I had an unshakable poker face, a stern disposition, but I had to behave in a certain way for men to take me seriously here. I had to be respected or I would be a target.

I'd learned that lesson long before I came to Nobody.

But Blake wasn't alone when he came through the swinging doors, and he didn't look especially jovial about it. But when he looked up at me, his scowl transformed to regret and that didn't make a lot of sense to me. First, he was a vampire. I didn't think they had a lot of capacity for regret. Second, I knew him which meant I knew those things were true.

But then I saw the man who strolled in behind him. The load on my heart lightened and I looked away then right back just to make sure I wasn't dreaming.

Time seemed to slow. Could it be?

Uncle Silas!

I slid off my barstool and raced to the front of the saloon and flung myself at my uncle. It wasn't lady-like or even adult, but it was true emotion and seeped from me. I couldn't believe it.

My uncle was in Nobody.

"What are you doing here? How?" I rapid fired more questions I wasn't even sure made sense because my mouth wasn't processing as quickly as my mind. My mind knew what had just happened to Uncle Silas and what it meant that he was now standing before me.

He couldn't go back. Couldn't resume his normal life. Would never see his home again.

Ever.

I glanced at Blake who had the decency to look as if he was sorry for what he'd done. But it wasn't enough. I glared at him. "Why would you do this?" My voice wasn't shrill, it was actually soft, but there was no mistaking the anger. A deaf man could've heard it.

But it wasn't just anger. It was betrayal. A second betrayal—it had happened before when Blake had brought me through The Rift. Now he had brought Uncle Silas.

I was really to claw his eyes out, to hurt him in a way it would take a long while to heal, and when he did heal, be ready to hurt him again, but Silas moved between us. "It wasn't his fault, Claire. I forced him to bring me to you."

But he didn't know the consequences of what Blake had done. He couldn't know. "You don't know. This is..."

"It was my decision, Claire. I sold the business and the house. There was nothing to keep me in Boston. You were the only reason I'd stayed there as long as I did." He spoke as if coming across The Rift was the most natural thing in the world.

I realized that the saloon had gone silent, and I turned to see everyone staring. I clenched my hands then motioned to the girls. "This is a private matter. Get back to what you were doing!"

The piano started back the clinking music and SarahBeth hollered for the people to gather to see her latest dance. And of course they did because she was a lot more interesting than I was. As if in slow motion, the saloon began to move again, and people turned away from the spectacle I was causing. Cherry floated by and took care of the last couple of men staring, locking her arms with theirs and escorting them off to the bar for fresh drinks, her skirts and petticoats rustling.

I turned to Uncle Silas. I was torn between the joy of seeing him and a deep despair that he wasn't going to ever see Boston again. Or his friends. How would he be able to handle that?

"Uncle Silas..." I needed to tell him. Needed him to understand he could never go back, and that the world here wasn't safe. Not for anyone.

"You don't need to worry, Claire. I'll be okay."

"But I don't think you understand." I pleaded with my voice, but I wasn't sure how else to explain the seriousness of his decision to him.

"This was my choice. I bought the supplies I thought I would need and tracked down the Pony Express station you used to mail your letters." He shrugged. "Then it was just a matter of waiting for you to send one." He looked back at Blake. "I forced him to bring me to you."

I looked at Blake. "Did you tell him? Did you..."

"I did." Blake clipped his words.

He told him but didn't spend much time on it. That, or he didn't give Uncle Silas the full picture of what was happening. Blake shrugged.

When I looked back at my uncle, he was smiling, and I smiled back. I should've known he would track me down. Should've expected it. He would want to make sure my "husband" was treating me right and no number of letters from me would convince him. He'd need to see it first handed. If he discovered I wasn't being treated well, said "husband" would end up in a pine box six feet below the earth in some bone orchard that no one visited.

It wasn't really Blake's fault that Silas was so protective of me. Silas would've forced him, wouldn't have given him time to explain the issue with The Rift or the dangers to humans on this side of it. I couldn't blame Blake.

Not entirely.

Instead of keeping them here out in the open in the saloon, we needed to get some privacy, some time for conversation and understanding that was away from the prying eyes of anyone who might have been a spy for the Fae King. I didn't know who to trust, so I didn't trust anyone except my employees and Blake.

I looked back at Cherry, who'd brought the guys to a nearby table to drink. "Watch this place for me. I'll be back later on." Then I glanced at Max, the bartender who was busy drying glasses and watching the rowdy crowd react to SarahBeth. "Back Cherry up, please."

The saloon would be fine. In fact, Cherry and Max were always trying to get me to leave them in charge and take a night off. It was hard to do, knowing that I had so much preparation for when we had to go for more rescues or to go after the Fae King. That day was coming.

I glanced at my uncle then at Blake. "Let's go back to my place where we can talk." I would have to tell him everything. And Uncle Silas would dissect every word, every sentence, and I would need Blake to verify. I couldn't believe that Blake had told him the important part—that he wouldn't be able to leave.

If he had, why would Silas be so happy?

It was going to be a long evening.

8

CLAIRE

Silas rode the path between the saloon and my house while Blake and I walked, Sunshine in tow. The sky was more vibrant tonight than usual, and the stars seemed closer, but such were things on this side of The Rift. Here the sky wasn't just blue. It was vivid, closer to a deep and vibrant purple. The sunset wasn't just rose and gold, it was every color of the rainbow—sometimes at once. The moon wasn't just bright and pocked, it was a giant orb, nearly full to bursting and close enough I could've reached to touch it.

We moved in silence, all of us knowing there

were serious discussions to have. I was so close to Blake, I could feel the heat from his body, and I was content in the moment just to walk alongside him, knowing he was there.

Silas waited to speak until the house was in sight. "That's your place? A little big for one person, isn't it?" He held his horse in place.

From this distance, the house looked bigger than it really was, and it *was* really big. "The guy who owned the saloon was corrupt. He had a big house and now it's mine." I shrugged. I left out a lot of details, but I had to figure out the best way to tell him. Later.

Neev met us at the hitching post out front and took Sunshine's reins from Blake and then Silas's horse—a coral mare with a coal black mane and ears that looked like they'd been dipped in ink.

He smiled at me. "Good evening, Miss Claire."

"Good evening, Neev." I looked at my uncle and nodded toward Neev. My little elven friend was beaming. Though he was scared of them, he loved new people, especially ones who'd never had a run-in with the Fae King. He loved hearing their stories and talking to them about everything. And Silas had plenty of stories, so he'd be in for a treat. Plus, since I'd brought Silas here, Neev wouldn't be as afraid.

"Uncle Silas, this is my very good friend Neev. Neev, this is my Uncle Silas."

My uncle stared to the point it was almost rude. I nudged him and he held out his hand to Neev. "Those are some fine ears you have."

Awkward, too.

I smiled at Neev who rubbed one of the points. "They're not fully in yet. I have a couple years of growing left to do. Nice to meet you." Neev switched hands to handle the reins.

Silas nodded and pulled his hand back. He looked at it as if he expected to find it gooey or slimy, but then he smiled. "You seem like a fine young man, Neev and I'm glad to meet ya."

Neev smiled like Silas had just called him President of the territory. "Thank you, sir. I look forward to talking to you later. Have a nice evening." He turned then led the horses toward the barn. Silas had complimented him in the best of ways, and there would be plenty of time to tell stories and become friends later.

Blake scanned the area for any threats. I don't think he ever took time off from being on alert. I'm not quite sure how he thought I got along before I met him.

Silas glanced at me. "Blake told me about this...

world, on the way to the saloon, but it's just now starting to make sense." He chuckled. "A whole new world."

I nodded. It certainly was. Even if Blake told him every story of every creature on this side of The Rift, no way was Silas going to believe him until he saw it himself. That was the problem with knowing all the things he knew. He was rarely tricked.

One of the things humans knew without being told was that the non-human creatures they'd heard stories of weren't real. Unfortunately, there was no reason to believe otherwise until you were on this side of The Rift.

Or so they thought. I'd thought so, anyway.

"It's just a little different." He could see it for himself. Probably already had.

"Oh, he told me. I didn't believe it until I tried to go back across, and it was like…" He shook his head as if he couldn't believe what had happened. "Like there was a wall in my way. Only I couldn't see it, so I just kept bouncing off it. I couldn't go through it, no matter how hard I tried." He paused. "Then Blake went back for my horse and my supplies, and just walked through that invisible wall."

Oh yeah. I knew the disbelief. Knew it like I

knew my own name. It took a minute to get over, too. To understand that being here was forever and if I hadn't had Blake to get the letters to and from Uncle Silas, I might not have survived.

"I know about the wall." I led them inside to the sitting room. This was the kind of conversation that required a drink, so I walked straight to the cart and poured two tumblers of whiskey. Blake wouldn't need one, so I handed Silas a glass and held mine, but I looked at Blake. "How, with all of your skills, did you manage to let a human sneak up on you?"

He smiled like he had secrets, but then he glanced away. "I was hungry. Too hungry to think, apparently."

Oh. I didn't have an answer for that. But once again, my feelings were all in my way of a conversation. I pushed them back and ignored the tingle in my belly. It didn't matter that he was staring at me with dark eyes. Didn't matter that part of me wanted to explore... thing with him. Crazy things. Things that made me wistful and wanting.

I sighed as he stood. He glanced at Silas then at me. "I'll let you two have some time to catch up. I need to check in with the Riders."

He tipped his hat to my uncle and made for the

door like he'd caught his pants on fire. I looked back at Silas. "I'll be right back."

If he noticed my trembling hands or the quiver in my voice, he didn't mention, and I loved him all the more for it.

I caught up with Blake in the foyer just as he turned the knob to the front door. I touched his shoulder and he turned. My mouth went dry, and I twisted a hand into the fabric of my skirt. It was long and black lace, would be wrinkled where I grabbed it, but I needed the anchor. "I'm sorry I was angry with you earlier." I'd blamed him when I should've known Silas didn't give him a choice.

His smile was everything. "Nothing to be sorry for."

He was graceful and gracious, like always. Those things made me like him more than I wanted to, more than I could help. I stepped closer to him, into his personal space, looked up at him and laid my hand on his chest.

"Thank you for bringing Uncle Silas here safely." Even if I wished Silas hadn't crossed The Rift, he had. If he hadn't done it with Blake, he would've found someone to bring him across and that someone could've been dangerous. Could've been Clayton or some other spy for the king.

Silas was stubborn and if he had his mind set on coming to find me, then he wouldn't be stopped.

And now he was here in my house. I hadn't realized how much I truly missed him until I laid eyes on him.

"You're welcome."

"Being busy is no reason not to eat." Neither was doing things for me, but I didn't mention that. I needed to sort through all the things I felt for him, all the things I wanted that I was too afraid to admit that I wanted. He was a vampire, for goodness sake.

"I'm fine, Claire. I'll..." He stared for a second, his pupils dilating as he looked at me. "Be fine."

He would never ask me, but the look said it all. His eyelids fell to half mast and his lips parted ever so slightly. He wanted to feed from me. Even if he wasn't about to ask.

And I wanted him to.

But right now, I had so many things to set in motion before I could worry about me or what I wanted.

I nodded at him and waited until he was out the door before I allowed the tears to escape. I watched Blake trace his steps and check the house, again, for any risks, then head to the barn to get Sunshine. I locked the door and dried my eyes, then turned to go talk to my uncle.

It was time to get him up to speed on what had really happened after I got off the wagon train.

9

BLAKE

Being away from her uncle had weighed on Claire as much as if she'd started carrying a boulder as a necklace against her chest. I was glad Silas had shown up near The Rift, and even gladder that he was taking all this so well. Some humans lost their minds when they discovered the difference between this side and theirs.

Especially after they found out they could never return to their side.

Silas didn't appear to be that kind of guy. He really seemed to be okay with the situation.

Having him here seemed to make Claire better, lighter. She was such a strong force and the feelings I had for her—whatever they were—were also strong. It was good to see her happier and a bit less stressed.

I was glad she was here in Nobody, but sorry that she'd been tricked to crossing The Rift. I was even sorrier for my part in the whole thing. But now that she was here, I couldn't imagine my life without her. I hoped that the familiarity of having her uncle here with her would give her some peace.

She always spoke so highly of him, and he'd obviously had a huge impact on her upbringing. He'd taught her so much.

After I left Claire with her uncle, I called a meeting of the local Riders. Riders Claire had likened to the otherworld's Pony Express, which of course they had compared themselves to as well. The thought made me smile. A lot of thoughts about Claire made me smile.

Aaron and a few of the others were already gathered inside when I walked in. Mostly, it was the Riders who were tired of the Fae King's hateful acts and domination over the land this side of The Rift. It was the guys who'd committed to fighting with Claire and many who'd already helped out.

Initially, I'd been afraid of the local Riders remaining neutral, or worse yet, splitting allegiance. The conflict with the fae was getting bigger and soon there would be no choice but to fight back or give in, and I needed to make sure everyone was with us. All it took was one dissenter to come along and say enough was enough and then the whole group could be in jeopardy. The king already didn't like anyone challenging his power—even imaginary challenges.

If Riders were seen as actively standing up to him, he'd unleash a full war on the area, and we weren't ready to deal with that. Not yet.

Everyone was seated and waiting. Aaron passed around a flask that could've been whiskey if he wasn't a vampire. Instead, it was blood.

I walked to the front of the room of the building that was like a city hall building on the other side of The Rift. There were benches set up like pews in a church, and a podium at the front. I'd talked to every single one of the Riders individually over the last weeks, and touched base with the general plan, but I needed to let them know the specifics.

Things were getting even more real.

"Claire Lowell is going to go from town to town to see who she can rally to help us." I hoped I didn't have to say it, but just in case, I also wanted it to be very clear. "We're going to fight the Fae King and put an end to the human kidnapping and breeding system he's set up. He's hurt a lot of people and we're going to put a stop to it, one way or another."

I looked at each Rider. These were the ones I trusted, but somehow the Fae King was getting information and a lot of it.

"There's a traitor in our ranks. Someone working for the Fae King or selling off information to one of his people. He keeps finding out where the surrounding towns and villages are, and we keep having to send the witches to shield and ward them again. It takes a lot to keep them all hidden." Nods and murmurs rumbled through the crowd. "As you probably know, we need to be on the lookout for Clayton. He isn't dead and there's no telling what he's planning or who he might've rallied to his side. We know that he will expose us, and he will give up information. We have to stop him."

I paused to let the information settle in the crowd.

Someone spoke up. "Why should we care about the humans?"

It was a valid question. "Today, it's the humans. Tomorrow, it could be the vampires. Who knows the limits of the Fae King's insatiable hunger for evil? In fact, he's already been using some of us. Why not take him out before he can mount an all-out war against our kind?"

The crowd buzzed, mostly in assent. I knew that risking our safety for humans could be a hard selling point for some, but any vampire who thought the Fae King wouldn't come for us at some point, had a very narrow vision.

"Hey, Blake. Why should we follow this woman?" Harrison Winchester—a new vampire who'd yet to have to live through a war or suffer through a plague hollered from the back of the room.

I nodded. There was always one in every crowd. "You're not following her. You're fighting beside her against a tyrant who uses, enslaves, kills." I shoot him a powerful glare. I was still hungry and short tempered because of it. "Claire isn't just any human, either. She's braver than anyone I've ever met. Willing to fight a king who tried to make her his slave. She's smart." I didn't think about how I sounded. I just kept going. She was counting on me to get their support, and I realized I was as passionate about this cause as she was. "If we ever want to defeat this king, we have to all work together. Otherwise, we should all just turn ourselves in to do his bidding now, because that's what's going to happen."

There were nods and murmurs of agreement.

"I'm in." Aaron stood and took a few seconds to look at the other men in the room. "Come on, Riders. This is what we live for. If we want to be free and have the ability to live independently, we have to fight to take down this despot. Many of us have already been helping. It's time to go from dipping our toe in the water to jumping in."

More nods and murmurs, then clapping and vampires rising to their feet. I didn't see a single vampire abstaining—and that surprised me. Everyone appeared to be fully onboard with supporting the cause.

Relief washed through me. "As soon as I get the final details of Claire's plan, I'll make sure you all know. It won't be long though."

We didn't have any hope of success unless we raised an army, so the plan didn't really matter until we knew we had enough men to take on the king and his army. Fae magic was so powerful, it was going to take careful planning to defeat it.

I wanted to tell the Riders that I wouldn't blame them for choosing not to fight, but the truth was, I would blame them. I would be angry. So long as the king was in charge, the life each of us wanted would be denied and the humans on this side of The Rift would always be in danger. And truly, not just the humans—but the elves and the pegasusi. And the vampires. And we'd probably find out many more had been enslaved by the king who thought everyone else was at his bidding and whim.

He thought he could make anyone bend to his will, especially young human women.

I wouldn't let that happen.

CLAIRE

I took Silas up to the saloon. He needed a drink and I wanted to check on a few business things. Though I trusted Cherry to keep things running smooth, there were nights that it took all of us to keep tempers from flaring. Those nights, Max earned his pay. They all did.

I had become used to being at the saloon and it felt like a home away from home. I knew I'd be leaving it soon, at least for a while.

On the other side of The Rift, I wouldn't have worried so much, but on this side, I was dealing with magic and shifters and vampires. It was a lot of power to put in an alcohol-filled room. I was lucky there hadn't been a major issue since I'd taken over.

We walked into the Dusty Bunny and there were more folks than usual at the table and in the stools on the front side of the house and bar. Not just the regulars, but a lot of people from town who had presumably come to meet Uncle Silas. Word had spread of a new human in town, and everyone wanted to see.

I hoped they'd all be buying drinks. That would be great for business.

I was still a novelty here in Nobody. It wasn't usual on this side of The Rift for humans to be in a position like mine. Not humans who weren't controlled by the Fae King. By association, Silas was also a novelty.

Joseph Hughes waved at me, and I waved back. He was a human who'd come across The Rift not looking for a wife but looking for *his* wife who'd been abducted from across The Rift. He'd hired a Rider—I wasn't sure which one—who'd taken a substantial amount of Hughes's money and brought him across. Although Hughes had never found his wife, he hadn't stopped looking. He'd settled in with the notion he wasn't going to be able to go back and now he fit right in with the people living here.

Then there was Jonathon Prior. Lars Ericson. A

human woman named Esperanza who'd been spending a lot of time with Jedediah Olson whose wife was promised a cure by Clayton if she only came across The Rift. She'd died before they ever made it to The Rift and Olson had gone too far looking and hadn't been able to get back. It only took one step too far and that was it. He didn't even get to go to her funeral.

Bottom line, the town was full of humans who'd been lied to, cheated, or had escaped from the Fae King's men before they were delivered. Several were women my team rescued. A rag-tag bunch but living their best lives right now.

As long as the Fae King didn't figure out where the town was hidden. It was always a risk.

The Fae King had no interest in human men except to build the numbers in his army, but they seldom lived to fight under his rule. He didn't like the competition. For whatever reason, fae women preferred human men. At least, the king's women did, and that certainly didn't please him. I'd learned all this information second hand but had no reason to doubt it.

I ignored them all for the time being. There would be time later for them to exchange stories with Silas, but right now, I wanted a drink and Max was working his magic behind the bar. Literally. He was a witch who had three or four bottles of liquor floating as he poured a line of shots.

Silas looked from me to Max, his eyes wide. "This really is a different world, isn't it?"

I nodded and introduced him to Max. "Max this is my Uncle Silas." They shook hands. "Max is a witch-human hybrid." He was also quite the novelty for the humans in the building who always watched his impressive displays of bartender showmanship.

"And Blake is a vampire?" Silas cocked a brow at me.

I nodded, but it was Max who took over the story. "Sadly, I'm not as long-lived as my father."

"Witches, unlike fae and vampires, only live a couple hundred years longer than humans. Max's life expectancy is about the middle of that." I'd done my research. The more I knew, the safer I felt. I imagined it would be the same for Silas.

He was busy digesting, quirking one brow then the other and the range of facial expressions he displayed would've been comical had I not known the exact stress of being in this situation. It was why I'd sought out information. Sharing the information I'd found out was the least I could do for him.

Before he had it worked out enough that his face

relaxed, Cherry walked over. "Silas, this is Cherry. She's my right-hand woman and she's engaged to Max."

Cherry's skin turned as red as her name, and she held out her hand for Silas. "I don't know about right hand, but I do know that Claire saved my life." Now it was my turn to flush. I had done what anyone in my situation would do. I'd saved her from the captivity and abuse of the Fae King.

My uncle looked at me then at the saloon. "I'm proud of you, Claire. This is a good business. You've done well for yourself and in such a short time."

"Thank you. My work here isn't nearly done. Taking down Donley was really just the beginning."

He nodded then reached inside his jacket pocket. "I almost forgot." He pulled out a pamphlet. *The Lily*.

It was a progressive paper that covered women's issues in today's society. I'd been reading it since I was a teenager.

My stomach sank just a little. With Silas on this side of The Rift, I wouldn't be getting any more papers. It was a small trade to have the man who raised me here beside me, though. I'd be okay.

I glanced through the paper, past articles and advertisements that seemed to come from another world, and then looked up, but Silas had already involved himself in a poker game with Olson and Hughes and a couple vampires who were hanging out, probably at Blake's behest.

I didn't know if it was true, but thinking it warmed me from the inside out.

Silas won his first hand, and Cherry chuckled beside me. "I can tell he's your family."

I nodded. There were similarities a blind man would have been able to see. "Yes, well, with Uncle Silas here, things will definitely be a bit livelier."

Cherry grinned. "I'm not sure the town can handle the both of you."

"Not like it has much of a choice."

CLAIRE

The entire town turned out for the meeting. Every pew was full and several of the men were standing along the wall so that the place would've probably exploded if one more person tried to enter.

They were taking turns discussing which also meant picking apart my plan for defeating the Fae King, Hughes, the same guy who'd been so excited to meet my uncle and drink my free rounds of whiskey at the saloon, stood in the center of the crowd and said, "We don't even know if we can trust her."

That was all acting Mayor Albert Jacson needed as encouragement. "Even if as according to Miss Lowell, Donley was a traitor and a man who helped the Fae King take women for his own nefarious purposes, John Donley was a businessman and the mayor of our town." He looked at me as if he thought I was solely responsible for Donley's disappearance. "We don't even know if he's dead or alive."

I hadn't known at the time the Donley situation occurred that he was the mayor, and his disappearance would make Jackson the mayor until an election could be held. Turned out to be a rather unfortunate situation.

Several heads turned in my direction and I kept my face blank and steeled against emotion, cards close to my chest. I hoped there wasn't going to be some kind of vigilante justice like the wagon train dispensed. I felt the heat of the men's ire rising and I could understand how it could get out of control.

I glanced at Blake who remained silently standing against the wall next to one of his vampire friends. It was hard not to look at him, not to keep looking at him, anyway. But I tore my gaze away and listened to the meeting going on around me. It wasn't going as I had hoped it would.

The men of this town were in a deep discussion about whether or not I was trustworthy. I sighed. I'd spent all these months trying to show them that I cared about the town and yet many of them still though of this as some type of publicity stunt to line my pockets or advance my own political leanings.

The fact it was the men putting me on mock trial made me angry, but I couldn't show it because that would give them what they expected—someone who was acting rashly from emotion. Nevermind that I'd saved a bunch of human women from sexual slavery, not the least of which was helped by the "upstanding" mayor of the town.

I could spit nails.

Jackson looked at me, as much malice in his eyes as I'd ever seen and shook his head like he was judging a demon from hell's depths. "You're very lucky, Miss Lowell. If not for the good that came of it, and fear that the Riders and the townspeople would revolt, I would have had you arrested." Heads shook and the low rumble of dissent began to wave from the back of the room forward. "Alas, you have escaped that fate."

Okay. Albert Jackson was not a man who was going to sing my praises. Fortunately, I didn't need his approval. Or for his fragile ego to validate me as a person. As long as most of the men here didn't feel the same way, I had a chance to bring them on to help me.

If not, then so be it. Let the fae find the town and burn it to the ground.

But now, it was my turn to talk, and people were looking at me. I stepped forward to the podium and surveyed the crowd. I reckon I'd not seen a group of unhappier people at a funeral. I glanced at Blake, and he flashed a big smile. He believed in me, and I believed in the cause I was fighting for. That was all that mattered.

I cleared my throat and spoke loud and clear, so there was no misunderstanding of my words or intent. "I know that the Fae King holds power, so much that we are forced to hide from him to save ourselves and our families. I think we should bring all the town leaders together and defeat this despot so we can bring our towns out of hiding permanently. No one should have to live in hiding, always afraid that they will be discovered."

This wasn't the entirety of the plan, but it was a component. And I probably should've explained more, but instead, I waited and listened. I gripped the edges of the podium.

Jackson stood, hands on his broad hips, forehead pinched, eyes narrowed. "She says that, but who's going to be assuming the risk? The Riders. The men.

Certainly not her." He looked me up and down like I was weak.

Oh, how little he knew about me. It took every bit of willpower I had not to challenge him to throw down in front of everyone in the room. But I needed to be a leader. I needed to appear strong and in control. I needed to not get rattled by inane comments from insolent people. My strength needed to show in my words right now. Words were my greatest power, and I knew how to use them. As long as I didn't get addled.

"I would stand beside any one of you and fight. Just as I did when I freed all those humans the king had imprisoned. I didn't run away. I stayed and fought." I narrowed my eyes and stood tall.

To them, I looked like one of *those* women. A hellraiser. A pot stirrer. A woman who would cause a ruckus then leave the mess for her "man" to fight it out and clean up. But that wasn't one bit of who I was at all. And that was certainly not a part of any plan I had. My intention was to be in the middle of the melee—and I dared anyone to try and stop me. If I could be the one to take down the Fae King myself, then all the better.

I was ready.

Uncle Silas stood. "Claire Lowell is a woman of

courage and intelligence. She was raised to fight injustices in the world and that means this world or the human one, same difference. If she says she's ready to fight, she's ready. How dare you question her intentions."

"More lip service from an outsider. Don't expect us to believe you." Jackson glared at Uncle Silas. But Silas was not a man easily intimidated by lip action and didn't back down one iota.

Uncle Silas nodded to me. "Claire can outdraw, outshoot, outfight any of you. She's a capable fighter and can go against any foe you can. I have no doubt she can take on this king you have."

I shrugged. There was no point in arguing. To my mind, either they believed in me as a member of their town, as a woman who helped stamp out the corrupt treachery that had been such a part of the town's fabric, or they didn't.

Nothing I said was going to sway anyone.

Silas scanned the room, taking in faces, measuring men's value by whether or not they sided with me or against me. If I was doing something of detriment, he wouldn't be so quick to judge them. Even for me. He had always been a straight shooter and he would never bend the rules for me or anyone else. "Is there a man here brave enough to challenge her? I say she can outshoot..." He took a pointed glance at Jackson. "You," then Oldson. "And you." Then Hughes. "You."

"I aint afraid of her. Or her shootin'." Oldson stood and tugged his pants up. "Let's do it."

"Yeah, let's see what the little lady can do. Either she's as good as you say, which I doubt, or you're as full of hot air as she is." Hughes leapt up and stood beside Oldson. "Somebody grab some cans from the kitchen. We're going to make a shooting statement out back."

I let out a deep breath. If a target match was what it took to get through to these men, then that's what I'd do. But it felt like a waste of time, and frankly, I was tired of having to prove myself worthy.

"You gonna join us, Jackson?" Oldson raised his voice over the din in the room as everyone talked about the shooting match.

Jackson nodded. "Wouldn't miss the chance to put her in her place." He turned and walked out of the room.

Blake pushed off the wall as if he was about to step in, but Silas held up his hand to stop him.

Silas was smart. He would never let me get hurt, and I wouldn't need anyone to rescue me. I could absolutely outshoot these men who would agree to the challenge just to keep form. They had no idea they were being set up. I could do this in my sleep.

The crowd dispersed. Or more accurately, went out back where the lawn behind the hall met the woods. I didn't like shooting blindly, or wasting bullets, but I couldn't step away from a challenge Silas had made on my behalf.

About a hundred and fifty feet from the back of the building, stood the stump of a tree that had probably been cut down for lumber to build the building. It was a good distance for a shooting match.

As two of the men set up some old tin cans on the stump, Blake moved to stand beside me. "If you don't want to do this, say the word and I will put an end to it. You don't have to prove anything."

But I did. If I outshot even one of these bozos, I wouldn't just be the woman who served them drinks —even though I'd never served a single one of them personally. I would be the woman who could outshoot them. Probably outride them and maybe even out fight them, though I wasn't itchy to prove that one.

I nodded at Blake. "It's nice of you to say, but this time, I do need to prove something. They need to trust that I'm not going to bail on the fight and that I mean it when I say we need to be a team."

For whatever reason, I wanted to reach out and pull him in for a kiss. I'd had such urges in the past, but never so strong and never so untimely, although I never acted. Wouldn't now either. I had a job to do.

He smiled and turned his body to face mine, and even tucked a strand of hair behind my ear. It was very forward to do in such a crowd and I should've objected but considering the thoughts in my head at the moment, this was a very chaste act.

Up close, he was better, more beautiful than he was at an appropriate distance, and my breath hitched. I had as many reasons to like him and be grateful to him as I did to be angry, and I didn't want to be angry.

I stayed next to him as the men finished setting up the targets and doing whatever prep work they thought was necessary. If out shooting was what it took to convince them, then it would be easy.

Once the targets were set up Jackson shot first. He hit two of the four cans square in the middle and they flew off the stump and spun in the air before pinging as they hit the ground. A few in the crowd clapped for him but he scowled at them, and they stopped. Maybe he expected to hit all of the cans. Hughes hit one can so hard it nearly tore the tin in two. Olson hit three, the last one barely being grazed, yet still falling. He pranced around like he'd won some major horse race or election.

I ignored all of them.

Silas nodded at me as I stepped into position. I could do this with my eyes closed, but I knew better than to be lax in my preparation. Any simple error could cause the bullet to go astray. I held up a wet finger. There was no wind. No reason for my aim not to be true. I could've done any number of trick shots even, but I didn't want them to think I was trying to show them up. It wouldn't do me any favors to wound their pride more than I would by hitting the targets.

I took my time setting up the shots.

Once the cans were in place, I fired four quick rounds and knocked each can down, then slid my pistol back into its holster.

After a quick gasp from the gathered group, Olson and Hughes congratulated me, but Jackson sneered. I didn't need praise, I needed action.

"I'll be in the thick of it. I'm not going to bail." I spoke to the three men specifically, but to the crowd generally. I hoped the demonstration was enough.

I walked back inside among the crowd and made my way to the podium. When everyone had taken their seats again, the women were sitting a little taller and most of the men were less adversarial toward me. At least, they weren't openly glaring anymore.

"I'm going to travel to all the towns and speak to the leaders about our mutual problem. We have to band together if we're to have a chance at all to defeat the fae and depose the king. For right now, it's only going to be talking and gathering information, but we need to know if there's hope or not. And then we can make specific plans."

I couldn't say how many of these folks believed in me or trusted that I was on their side. All I'd been able to show them was that I could shoot well and speak to a crowd. Hopefully, that was enough for them to want to be on my side and at least give me the chance to work on the plan to take out the king.

I owned a business in this town, so I had as much a stake as anyone if the wards went down and the Fae King found out where we were. I'd lose everything. It was why I'd called this meeting. Plus, I had ties to the Riders. I understood the issue with the townspeople. They didn't want another shakeup. They wanted reassurance that the saloon was in good hands. Some of them wanted to pretend there wasn't an issue at all, that we were safe from the fae.

Most knew that was a ruse, and it was a matter of

time before we had to deal with the fae directly again.

The opposition to banding together with the other towns came from the greedy and the scared. The weak. They were the ones who were concerned about profits over people. But without people there would be no profit. I had to hope they could look past their own fears and insecurities, around their avarice and meekness to seeing that.

If we didn't stick together, we'd go down one by one.

"I'm asking for your support. For you to not give up on us, on this town, but to be ready to defend her if necessary. On everything that we can be if we take on the Fae King and win." There were people nodding, some not moving, and others who were just staring. I couldn't read the whole room.

I stared at Blake. He smiled and nodded, and his confidence meant a lot to me, but I needed their support. All of them. Or at least most of them.

I waited while they discussed and talked over the issue. When Jackson asked for a vote, I waited some more, hoping against hope they would side with me and give me the support I so dearly needed. There was nothing I wouldn't do to protect this town and my saloon.

If I had to do it without them, it would be harder, but what choice did I have.

The vote came in almost unanimous. The townspeople would support me. I felt like I had won the biggest prize of all. I guess I hadn't realized how tenuous my confidence was. Knowing I had the support of the people of Nobody gave me the extra boost I needed.

I was going to raise an army and we were going to defeat the Fae King.

After packing, I headed to the Bunny to see Uncle Silas and Cherry and the rest of my crew. They'd have to tend the place while I was gone, and since Uncle Silas had just arrived in the sanctuary so I wanted to spend as much time with him as I could before I had to leave.

BLAKE

I wasn't only surprised, but happy that Claire had asked me to be her guide on the trip. I hoped it meant she trusted me, but the only indication was that she'd asked. I couldn't be sure, only by the feeling in my gut and certain looks she gave me, but I was almost sure she was still holding a grudge for my part in her being stuck here, and now her uncle, as well. It was unfortunate, but there was nothing I could do about it.

Sunshine plodded along the trail with the other horses, being more amenable than usual, which was a great change of pace,

I felt bad about her being stuck but that was compounded by being glad she was stuck here on this side with me. I had a lot of mixed feelings when it came to Claire. I had a hard time remembering my life before she was in it.

For his part, Silas loved "a good adventure," and he'd taken to looking at this as the biggest one he'd ever been on.

Better than Boston, he'd told me just after he'd also told me not to blame myself. I was doing a job I was paid to do by bringing Claire here, and he'd pointed a gun at me to make me bring him here so he could see her. *Can't fault a man for making a living or trying to save his own life.*

Of course, he was also the man who'd said, *What better adventure than taming the wild west–the* magical *wild west.* His eyes had lit up and I'd chuckled. To them it was magic. To me it was life.

But Claire was angry about her uncle being stuck here, and I could see it. She made sure I did, too. There'd been plenty more sighing than her usual amount since Silas arrived, though she was glad to see him, too.

Peggy nickered and shook his head, probably because there were still miles of trail left before we would get to Amberhill. He wasn't a rider horse that was used to this kind of workout. Plus, he probably wanted to spread his wings and fly, but we couldn't take that kind of chance while we were on our way to a town hidden from the Fae King. Claire leaned forward and rubbed his neck and he smiled.

The flying horse smiled. I must have imagined it.

I glanced at Claire. She looked at me and didn't glare so I guessed we were making progress. She even smiled with a pretty blush creeping up her cheeks. It was the same smile she'd given me when we were on the trail before I brought her across The Rift. It made me feel like a heel.

"It's dark tonight. Darker than usual, it seems like. Even with the moonlight." Her voice was soft, silky, like fabric brushing over my skin. She held Peggy's reins lightly, giving him the lead. He started prancing, kicking his knees up high and bouncing Claire.

I nodded. It wasn't so much that I was a man of few words–I was–but more that I didn't have anything to answer that wouldn't sound awkward. Best not to answer. So, I didn't.

But I liked the way she spoke and how sometimes the words dripped from her tongue like honey. Also *that* she spoke.

"Thank you for agreeing to accompany me." Again, the softness of her voice made my stomach clench and my body go tight.

"I'm..." What was I? "Happy to do it.

"Peggy!" Claire strained. "Stop that." She took the reins a bit tighter and settled Peggy into a more relaxed walk.

What had gotten into that feathered horse?

When I'd asked who she was traveling the trail between the hidden towns with, and she'd said it was her plan to bring me and a couple others, I'd been surprised and not hid it very well. *Are you sure you want to travel with me?* I couldn't blame her if she didn't trust me. I wouldn't if I was her.

If I was one of her advisors, I would have told her not to trust me either, even though I would take a dose of pure west sunshine before I hurt her again. As long as my life was, I'd spend every day of it still feeling the pangs of guilt for what I'd done.

But she'd looked at me like my accompanying her was a foregone conclusion. Like she expected I'd be by her side. That felt good.

"Did you feed before we left?" Her voice was that soft purr again, and I smiled at her, held her gaze for a couple steps because Sunshine knew how to stay on a path. I wasn't sure how well she could see me in the darkness, but I could see her react.

Behind us, Aaron Drakeborne, another vampire, and Crystal, a witch who helped put the new markers and wards in place, rode silently. They didn't have a lot in common, although neither did Claire and I, but we managed small talk, at least.

I, for one, was glad Crystal decided to ride with us. It was convenient when we made camp because she could up wards that would shield us from intruders and anyone who might try to interfere. The extra protection made me worry a little less about Claire.

We were on our third night of travel already and we made camp under the twinkling stars. Close by, a twig snapped, or that was what it sounded like, but it was actually the crackling of a ward that had been touched. Light flashed in tiny bursts of color. We were warned.

I stepped out of my tent and looked toward where Claire and Crystal had pitched theirs on the other side of the fire. Their lantern was bouncing through the woods when Drakeborne came out of his tent.

A faebeast wasn't a challenge to a couple vampires, but they would be dangerous to the women we were with. Claire was human and faebeasts loved the taste of humans as much as I hated the taste of faebeast. Especially fae feline.

This one was huge. Its eyes glowed a deep red and its mouth opened with a hiss to reveal rows of jagged teeth sharp enough to tear apart flesh and bone with little effort. This beast was bulky—probably a male—and covered in small spots. In the dark, I wasn't sure what color it was. It was more than large enough to be deadly.

I motioned for Aaron to circle behind it. He moved, slow and silent. Of course, he had to go beyond the ward to come behind it, but the wards were a shield only equipped with a warning.

Before he could pounce, and since he was a Drakeborne, that only meant he hadn't chosen to pounce yet not that he wasn't fast enough, a shot rang out and the beast fell. When the smoke from the shot cleared, Claire was standing with her rifle on her shoulder.

Crystal flexed her magic fingers to send the big cat to magic oblivion. It was too dangerous to leave him lying in plain sight. If one of the king's spies saw it and reported back, it would give away our location. Could expose Amberhill's location or at least the trail it's on and that would be problematic.

Looked like the ladies had taken care of things on their own. I really shouldn't have doubted them in the first place.

Aaron glanced at me, and I shrugged. I'd assumed she'd brought Aaron and me along as her protection from things that posed a danger, but now, it was grossly apparent that she didn't need us nearly as much as I thought she would. I felt like I had learned the same lesson before.

Before I could ask any questions, Claire had retreated to her tent and Crystal was headed for hers.

By morning, as Claire cleaned her gun and Crystal whipped up breakfast, they sat in front of a fire. "I've only met one other witch," Claire said. "Are you born witches? Or is it a skill?"

Crystal looked at Claire over her shoulder. Considered her for a second. "The ones who are taught magic aren't true witches, although sometimes, they're better at the craft." She shook her head at Claire and tendrils of her long auburn hair escaped from her braid. She tucked an errant curl behind her ear then toyed with a blue crystal pendant she wore on a strap of leather around her neck. "The Fae King teaches them. If he finds them worthy."

"He sure seems to think he knows a lot." Claire quipped.

Crystal held the skillet still and spoke without turning. "He thinks he knows everything."

"Well, we're going to have to educate him,"

Claire said. "And I think I know a few teachers who'd be perfect for the job."

As I watched her, Claire glanced at me once or twice and smiled like she'd done when we first met. This felt a lot like those times, and I couldn't say I minded.

13

CLAIRE

I didn't think, after what happened the last time I traveled, that I would enjoy another trip, but traveling across this realm, so far, was actually quite fun. Maybe because I was getting a break from daily drudgery at the saloon, or maybe it was the company. I'd never really had the opportunity to get to know a witch, since none existed—that I knew of—in Boston. And Crystal was the first I'd had the chance to spend much time with on this side of The Rift. Shaleena came into the saloon, and I liked her, but I didn't get to talk to her about witchy things. She was more distant. Crystal felt like a sister.

I genuinely liked her.

I'd brought Peggy along with me, but left Neev at home with my uncle. He wasn't happy about being left behind, but he wasn't the kind of boy who was prone to complaint. He'd been captured by the king once, and I didn't want to risk him again, even if it meant he was unhappy.

Besides that, Uncle Silas promised to teach him *a thing or two,* which meant by the time we returned, Neev would probably be an accomplished rider, a master shooter, and he would be knowledgeable about all things human. Silas always said that knowledge was power, and he firmly believed in spreading his around. My sweet little elf boy was going to end up being a hard drinking, gun fighting, poker player.

As we rode, Peggy veered toward Sunshine. Again. Sunshine nipped at him, and he pulled back. She ignored Peggy as much as she could, and even pushed him away when he got too close. He didn't seem to ever take the hint.

He slowed, pouting, wings down. I would've laughed, but I knew the feeling. Not that it was anyone's fault but my own.

I knew I'd been punishing Blake for nothing. Well, it wasn't nothing, but it wasn't his fault either.

The west, and I knew it, was full of dangers and things I hadn't expected or understood. The Rift with him–especially now that Silas was here–was probably safer than anything I would have encountered on my own on the other side.

Now, he was forgiven. I was doing everything I knew to do to let him know. Smiles. Gentle speaking. Brushing touches when I could manage.

Because I'd been so harsh, he was blaming himself for bringing Uncle Silas through. The truth was, I was glad Silas was here, glad we'd been reunited. And I was under no such illusion that Silas had given Blake a choice. Silas Lowell didn't operate like that.

Thanks to Blake, I'd been considering writing a book about this world and sending it through with him to the other world. *Thanks to him.* It made me like him more that this world opened a whole different set of choices to me.

We rode on through the day. The trail was rough, and we had to be careful, but Blake stayed close to me, as close as Aaron stayed to Crystal, and even though we had to be careful not to draw attention, we covered a lot of ground. We'd talked some to pass the time, but mostly we'd ridden in silence.

A couple Riders were coming toward us in the distance, and I moved Peggy closer to Sunshine, so it looked like I was "with" Blake. Better to look like a couple–and I didn't mind one bit– than for the Riders passing us to wonder why I needed a vampire escort. Riding beside him was no hardship.

Crystal rode behind me with Aaron beside her. I liked both of them, too. Crystal was a take no crap kind of girl. It was something I could respect, a commonality between us, but she smiled at Aaron and her cheeks flushed.

We were a few days on the trail by now, and this world continued to fascinate me. There were parts on the trail that I hadn't seen before and around every bend, new sights and smells met my senses. From vibrant colors of pollen to the desert flowers whose blooms opened and closed as if they were speaking and answering one another, the world felt like a place designed by artists and magicians.

A wonderland.

But when we came to an expanse of land that stretched in one direction as far as the eye could see, and in front of us for a few acres at least, the landscape changed. The ground was dark, almost black, and no greenery grew in any spot. The whole area was barren. Instead, what looked like bones the size of tree trunks protruded from the ground in all directions. Some pieces were broken and jagged and cast around in a haphazard fashion, and some looked to be whole. None looked familiar, really, other than they did seem like the remains of some enormous animals. I pulled Peggy to a halt.

I stared, trying to figure out what my eyes were seeing as Crystal stopped beside me.

"What is this?" I pointed to the field.

She paused then spoke. "It's a bone orchard of sorts. A reminder."

I stared. "What kind of bone orchard has bones that large?" I mean, it looked like bones, but I'd never seen ones that large. Ever.

"Dragons." Crystal spoke solemnly and in a low voice. "Those are dragon bones."

"Dragons?" Dragons were for children's stories. So were witches and vampires. Which meant that in this world, anything went. The need to get closer for an investigation and the urge to hide warred inside of me. "Are we in danger of a dragon attack?" I hated the waver in my voice. This was my mission, my expedition, and here I was, quivering, ready to take cover under a pegasus wing.

Blake's horse danced a few steps beside me before he brought her under control. "The last Fae King had all the dragons hunted and killed. He knew they represented a threat to what the fae wanted." His tone dropped to a low and angry murmur. "There's an ancient legend that says the dragons knew it was the fae opening The Rift between worlds. The fae and the dragons fought—at first it was the fae attacking but soon the dragons defended and many fae died. One of the dragons who'd survived the war killed the fae king and queen. Then the prince was crowned."

He'd told me some of the history of this realm before, and I'd picked up some of the lore at the saloon. But no one had ever mentioned dragons. This was all new. Unexpected, too.

I wasn't sure what to think. At some point I was going to have to stop being surprised at what I would see or hear in this realm.

I looked out over the field of scarred bones, my stomach quivering and bile rising in my throat. The place wasn't really a cemetery—it was the scene of a massacre. There was no order, no real burial or memorial. These bones were cast out onto the land to rot.

A warning beacon to anyone who dared to think they could stand up against the king of the fae.

A warning directed at me.

Why I felt it was a message for me, when I knew it had happened well before I was born, I didn't know, but as surely as I felt the heaving warmth of my living and breathing pegasus under me, this was a warning to me.

My conviction to return this world to a safe and free place for all creatures filled my heart and I felt the same sense of power I had felt the first time I had hit a small target at forty paces and surprised Uncle Silas with my ability. I'd surprised myself too.

I could do it. I would do it.

I turned to Crystal. "That prince, is that the current king?" I knew that fae had long lives, but I wasn't sure how many years we were talking about.

"Yes." Crystal rubbed her necklace then spun it on her neck and spit on the ground. "The king—the one we have now, Theska—rallied all the fae races. The war began again. Raged on." Crystal looked wistfully at the graveyard. "The dragons were useful, and good stewards of the land. They were powerful and heroic. But the king threatened anyone who allied with the dragons and forced them to fight on his side. He wiped out the entire dragon species in a short time."

It was a lot to take in. A whole species wiped out because of one jealous king. King Theska. I had not heard his name spoken before—but I knew that names held magic, so I wasn't surprised that he wasn't always called by his actual name. Crystal's necklace charm was proof she took the name seriously.

Knowing his name, for me, took away some of his power. I'd call him by his name because it made him feel more real to me, and somehow smaller.

The whole story was sad, too, and it added to the weight of the issue. But it gave me another little bit of information about the fae king that I didn't have before. Not that I needed it, but it also gave me another reason to hate him. It also made me wonder what threat he'd been able to find that would convince the allies to fight with him and turn on the dragons.

Even the dragons of folklore were majestic creatures of magic. Why would he want to wipe them out? He was really *that* petty and horrible that he'd kill them all?

The more things I knew about this King Theska,

the better I could prepare to fight him and the sooner I could defeat him and restore order and fairness.

I held my head and leaned forward on Peggy. Being around the bones made me woozy, like I'd been spinning around fast then dropped to the ground. No one else felt it, but Blake made sure to get me to comfort quickly.

We rode on, putting as much distance between us and the graveyard as we could.

14

CLAIRE

Amberhill was a lot like Nobody. It had a small church, a general store with farm implements in the window, a small school with a bell, a saloon, and a line of hitching posts in front of a row of buildings. A dirt road went smack dab down the middle and people milled about, sometimes dodging a horse or group of kids running by.

The whole place looked like small towns back home, except that some of the flora was different, and yeah, some of the fauna. No pegasusi around Boston. And definitely no dragon boneyards.

Men with wagons loading and unloading at the mill stopped working to watch us drive in. They continued watching as we dismounted, tied up our horses, and stood in front of the saloon's swinging door trying to figure out where to go. I didn't secure Peggy's lead—just pretended to. I was terrified someone would try to steal him, so I gave him the ability to fly away if someone did try. Otherwise, he knew to stay put.

Before we could walk into the saloon, a woman dressed in a shiny blue gown rushed out and threw herself at Aaron. He caught her and kept her from knocking them both to the ground. She squished her bosom against his chest and wiggled back and forth, then added a high-pitched squeal as she pulled him down for a very inappropriate for the company kiss.

It was a kiss I'd deem inappropriate for anyone you weren't actually kissing. And probably not appropriate for some you were kissing.

I nudged Blake but he was staring at Crystal whose scowl was deep, a permanent damage to the skin kind of scowl.

"Intriguing," I whispered, meaning the situation as much as the kind of kiss he was still getting. I wondered for a second if Blake would like to be kissed by this woman like that. I hoped not. My skin flushed with heat. I shouldn't have been thinking about kissing Blake, but I was. Right there in the street.

"Isn't it now?" He stared at me for a second, until my skin heated some more.

I wanted him to be thinking of kissing me the same as I was thinking of him, but even if he was, I wouldn't know what to do about it. That thought made the heat die.

When we turned away from each other, and I broke the gaze to look at Aaron again, he wrenched out of the woman's arms. He shot a sheepish look at me then at Crystal. "I can explain."

Crystal crossed her arms and smirked, and I figured she said enough for both of us. She shook her head, lifted her skirt, and strode past him and the woman into the saloon.

Aaron disentangled himself from the woman for a second time and chased after Crystal as another man came out of the saloon doors, his hand extended. "Hello, hello. Bradley Tuppin, Mayor of Amberhill. We don't get a lot of strangers round here. But we're sure glad you're visiting." He finally took a breath. "What can we do you for?"

They didn't get a lot of strangers in town because of the wards, and he surely knew that. It was by design. He was right to be suspicious of anyone who came to town, and his friendliness didn't hide his misgivings. He knew as well as anyone that people weren't just going town to town on vacation. It was too dangerous.

Usually, it was the Riders that were traveling between towns, carrying information, mail, and packages. They weren't quite so flamboyant about their entrance.

"Claire Lowell, and this is my associate Blake Rider. We're from Nobody."

I wondered why more people didn't look confused, but his one quirked brow was comical, and I chuckled. "Nobody the town. We're not too far from here." He nodded and the confusion faded, so I continued. "We're here to discuss some very..." I tried out a couple words–disturbing, troubling, worrisome—in my mind. "Concerning news. We're looking for help."

"Some help, you say?" He shot a look at Blake. "What kind of help might you need, little lady? I'm sure this young gentleman can tell me all about it while you get some rest and maybe a drink?"

I nodded. There was a certain comfort in knowing that things were the same in every world, and a certain amount of disappointment in the same. I looked at the mayor. Men like him were everywhere and there was nothing I could do about it right now, as much as it ate away at me. But I smiled at Blake and left him with the other man. I walked into the saloon.

Not unlike the Bunny, this place was alive with music–a piano player in the front corner–and dancing girls, poker players and ale and whisky drinkers. The floor was hardwood, beautiful red oak scarred by dancing and fighting, by the slide of a chair and any number of cups and bottles dropped and broken on its surface.

I took a seat at the bar, ordered an ale, and laid out money. It was a lot more than the drink cost. I was well aware of the benefit of befriending the bartender.

Fortunately, coin had remained the same throughout the realm even after the fae had locked things down. The bartenders appreciated money and tips and they were the men who knew all. Heard all. Served everyone and was therefore a friend to each of them. He was the man to talk to and money would make his tongue looser.

I smiled and tried to make myself pretty, the way the dancing girls did it at my saloon. I could've bought the information, wasn't above it, but I had wiles and I was suddenly interested in taking them out for a ride. I'd seen what the girl had done earlier—no I wasn't going to kiss the bartender—and now I wanted to sharpen my tools.

He looked at me with a hunger. I could only define it as a predatory glare, and all my senses prickled.

He was probably thirty or so, at least in human years. He wore a bow tie and a wedding ring, which seemed a bit odd given the magic that swirled around him. Something about him seemed off—like he held power that he might wield at any moment.

"I'm not from around here." I made my voice meek.

"I would remember." His smile was half leer, half smirk, like I wasn't quite temptation for him but also like he wasn't above taking advantage of what he perceived as my desperation.

I gave him another "pretty" smile and pushed a piece of hair behind my ear. "A friend and I are looking for another woman who said there might be jobs near here. Outside of town."

He shook his head. "Oh, little lady. A lot of women come through here. Not a lot of them stay. Why would I know anything about a job?" He was so smug I wanted to shoot the grin off his face, but I held on to my ruse.

"I guess I figured since you employ women, you might know of another place that had similar jobs nearby. Maybe you heard talk of a place." I was still playing it cool, but my stomach turned in on itself and did a disgusted roll.

"I might know a thing or two."

I sighed deep inside my soul but kept my smile plastered on my face. I tilted my head and leaned forward, having unfastened the button when he looked away. Apparently, my wiles were located a few inches south of my collarbone.

I leaned closer still and let him play a little peek-a-boo with my cleavage. After a second when he didn't speak, I sat back. No information meant no free peeking. "Like what?"

He chortled like he'd never seen a breast before then sobered as the saloon doors opened again. His voice fell to a near whisper. "There's a fae outpost nearby. I know some women have been seen around there but I'm not sure in what capacity."

Yeah, I was pretty sure they weren't getting paid. I cocked my head as Blake walked toward me. It wasn't so much that I saw him as I sensed him then looked back and there he was. His timing was impeccable.

He smiled and slung his arm around me then

pulled me closer to him. "Making friends?" he whispered into my hair.

The bartender lost interest and Blake looked down at me, way down, and his eyes went wide. "Claire!" He spun me toward him and looked from left to right. "You're exposed."

That I was. I fastened the shirt while he shielded me and tried to avert his eyes but failed. I smiled up at him, trying my wiles to cover my embarrassment. I wanted him not to look so horrified that he'd seen my cleavage. The woman in me wanted him to *want* to take a closer look. Instead, he stepped back as if even the thought of touching me was a bad idea, or at least one he didn't care for.

"We should get you and Crystal to the inn before the word gets too far that there is a new beautiful woman in town." His voice was husky, and he hadn't yet brought his gaze up from my collarbone area.

A warm flush of feminine power worked its way from my belly through the rest of my body. I wanted to curl up against him and let his body wrap around mine.

The urge was powerful, and I leaned.

"Are you all right, Claire?" He reached to put a steadying hand on each of my shoulders. "You look feverish." He moved one hand to lay it on my forehead.

"Oh." The skin-to-skin touch shot bolts of pleasure through my veins. What was happening to me? My body was acting of its own volition, and I didn't care for it. I stepped away and his arms dropped. "To the inn. Right. Yes, that's a good idea."

He'd just called me *beautiful*. It was a miracle I could think at all. That one remark would get me through a lot of lonely dark nights.

As we made our way to the inn, he walked beside me, not quite relaxed, but neither did he have his gun drawn or his fangs out. I'd never seen him so confused.

I didn't know how aware he was, but I'd noticed a man flanking us to my left. He wasn't even that hidden or sly. I looked at Blake, smiling, caught off-guard once more by how attractive he was, but just nervous enough to realize the urgency of the situation. We were being stalked.

"Blake, I think we're being followed." I gave the slightest nod I could toward the man still walking beside us.

The street was mostly empty, so it should've been pretty clear to Blake who I was talking about.

"I've been watching him." Blake moved to put

himself on the other side of me, between me and the man. He slid his gun out of the holster and slipped it to me. I held it close, but ready.

"This is going to happen very fast." His voice was low and more of a growl than spoken, but I heard it and I understood. He was going to use his vampire speed to take care of the situation. The gun he handed me was but a precaution.

My own weapons were in the bag he dropped as he took off after the man. I couldn't see him until he stopped moving. He was faster than my eyes could follow.

Blake dragged the man by his collar to stand in front of me. "Why are you following us, dirtbag?" Blake asked.

The man sputtered and grasped at his neck, and Blake straightened him, not letting go of his collar. I took a step back. I'd never seen the man before, but he seemed a few apples short of a basket—a crazy look in his eye that put a scare in me. Was he upset about us being in town? Or was there something more to his madness?

"I'm giving you one more chance before I separate your head from your neck," Blake said. "Why are you following us?"

"Miss Lowell." The man sputtered. I motioned

Blake to let him go, or at least give him more access to speaking. I still held the gun.

When Blake let him go, the man turned and smashed his fist into Blake's jaw.

I moved to stand between them. "Woah. Why all the violence?"

I was not deluded enough to think that Blake couldn't go through me to kill the man if he wanted to, but I couldn't just stand by and let it happen. There had to be a reason for such a reaction, and I wanted to know what it was.

The man held his fist at the ready and I sensed Blake about to strike.

"Who are you and what do you want?" I asked.

Not only did I not want to see Blake take the man's head off, but I figured it wouldn't be good for our relations with the townsfolk. If we wanted their help, we couldn't go around beheading them.

"Name's Joe Guthrie." He crouched, in a position somewhere between offense and defense.

Did he not realize Blake's abilities?

"Mr. Guthrie?" Blake clasped his hands.

Mr. Guthrie stared hard at Blake. "You remember me, you son of a bitch?"

If Blake had color in his face, it would've drained. His lips parted and his eyes lowered. "Mr.

Guthrie." He nodded. "Yes. I remember you." He looked at me, sheepish, regretful. Guilty. "I led them across The Rift."

I took a step back. Mr. Guthrie stood taller, and his posture grew...angrier.

"Ah." Now it made sense. I nodded at Mr. Guthrie. "I understand your anger. More than you realize." He probably had family on the other side, a life he hadn't meant to give up.

He looked at Blake. "Do you know what you did? Did you know then what you were doing?"

Blake rubbed his forehead like he had a headache. "I'm sorry."

"I should kill you right now. I've been waiting to see you, to have the chance. It's what you deserve."

I had to say something, stop this before it got worse.

"Mr. Guthrie." He didn't look at me but continued glaring at Blake. "Joe, please." I kept my voice soft, and he glanced at me. I placed a hand on his shoulder and held the gun behind my back. He startled at the touch. "Joe, Blake was doing a job."

"That bastard took my wife and my little girl. It's taken me a couple years to figure out how to get to this godforsaken place he brought them." He pointed at Blake and for a second, I wondered if Blake had done it, then I knew it had, and my stomach tightened. There was nothing I could do but empathize, get the rest of the story, and give him my word that I would do whatever I could to bring his family home.

But first, I needed all the details. And I needed to hear the entire story. "The Fae King?"

Blake nodded, spoke miserably. "Yes." He looked down. "They were part of a wagon train heading to California. I brought the women and children through The Rift."

"You're an evil bastard. I paid you to keep my family safe. Bring them to me." His voice choked on emotion, and he tried to go around me to get at Blake again.

I shoved him back and it took all the strength I had to do it. Not because I thought Blake needed protection, but because I needed to know the story. And I needed Blake *not* to act. If Blake did something, the situation would be irreversible.

"I'd already made a place for us in California. A beginning. Wasn't much, but it was ours. And you ruined it! Where are they now? This place is so crazy, and I can't find them anywhere."

He lunged again and I blocked him. Blake kept his head down. I hoped he was ashamed of what he'd done, but I didn't want him to hurt anyone or himself. He was already a better person but that didn't mean he didn't have to atone for what he'd done.

I hardened my tone and pointed at Guthrie. "If you know what he's done, you know who he is and that he can kill you without breaking a sweat." I didn't even know if vampires could sweat. Not that it mattered. I couldn't let Blake kill him. He'd suffered enough. It made me want to find his family. I hoped they were still alive.

Guthrie pulled back and adjusted his clothes again.

"Come to the meeting tomorrow. We're going to talk to the town about banding together. About freeing all those people the Fae King is holding." I paused. "We've already freed some. And we will keep trying until everyone is released."

Sad as I was to say it, there were probably a lot more stories like his. I wondered what the scope of it looked like.

It took a couple seconds of heated glaring at Blake before he glanced at me again and nodded.

"I'll be there. I hope you can find them." He dipped his chin and nodded. "Goodnight, ma'am."

"Goodnight." When I was sure Guthrie was gone, I looked at Blake. His eyes were dark, and he had the hunched shoulders of a man who was haunted by his past, by his misdeeds. I felt for him. I couldn't absolve him for what he'd done, but this quest we were on offered redemption, if nothing else, the chance to make up for all the wrongs he'd committed.

I couldn't help but wonder how many people he'd ferried across The Rift at King Theska's bidding. And what made him stop? If he thought it was okay to begin with, what had changed his mind?

I laid my hand on his arm. "Blake…"

He didn't shrug me off or push me away like I expected. Nor did he acknowledge that I was touching him. He simply stood. Shoulders hunched. Eyes downcast.

Then he looked at me, eyes burning. I couldn't tell if he was angry or sad or just hungry. "I should get you to the inn. Being out in the open is dangerous."

I nodded. There was no reason to argue. He was right. I walked beside him to the inn and when we reached the porch, he helped me up the stairs like I was a proper lady and he was a suitor, and oh, how my mind wished for just a second that things were that simple. In that second, it didn't matter what he'd done or what he was. I knew the man. I knew *who* he'd become. I knew he was gentle and kind, respectful despite all the atrocities to his name.

But when the time passed, I gave him one last smile, turned to the inn door, and walked inside. I couldn't console him. I couldn't change what he'd done. Couldn't provide absolution. All I could do was smile softly, let him know we were okay.

And that tomorrow we'd work on making things even better.

Blake came back to the inn in the morning. I wasn't sure he would, given how he'd left the night before. I didn't know the first thing about his emotions or his ability to pretend like Guthrie never approached us. It had stuck with me all night, and I didn't sleep until way after midnight.

"There's a fae outpost close by. It won't take us long to get there." He smiled and it was almost as if last night never happened. Except for the haunted shadows in his eyes, there was no outward effect of it anyway. "It's not well-manned, and with it being new, it will be an easy target."

I nodded because I liked the idea and I liked that he'd come to me with the idea. "Okay. That's probably the same place the bartender was talking about where he'd seen women around. Maybe there are some captives there."

"I think that's a fair assumption. Some of the Riders have volunteered to help check it out, and there are a lot more we can call on if we need them." He nodded and pulled an envelope from his pocket. "This came for you by Rider this morning."

I didn't ask how it had come here, to Amberhill, but only took it from his hand and broke the wax seal. Seals were an old way of securing letters and I'd given each of my girls a stamp and told them to use the seal so I would know it was truly from one of them and not a false message sent by an impostor.

I opened the envelope and pulled out the page. As I read, Blake watched me, smiling. "What does it say?"

I read the whole thing then went over the highlights a second time. "Says no traitors have been discovered. But some Rider scouts"—I glanced up at him— "Your guys, I guess, told the girl about the elf guardsmen. Ten or so." I might've looked like I had all the answers, a plan even, but I did not. I had an idea. That was all. "Your Riders have been working with the girls?"

He nodded. "They get the girls from town to town."

"I need to speak with them so I can thank them. To make sure they stay in service of the good, and to tell them I'll hire them to help us." I meant it to be a conciliation, but he shook his head.

"They aren't mercenaries who can be bought. They're Riders. Delivery boys." His voice was a bit strained.

Maybe I'd insulted him. I couldn't tell, but I didn't like the way his look changed.

"I know." I was appropriately remorseful, but his frown stayed in place. "Blake, I didn't mean it that way."

After a few seconds, he nodded. "I know." He glanced to his left then his right. "I'll take Aaron and we'll talk to as many Riders as we can. See if there's any more information that can help us."

He was a good man, and for a second I wondered about him, about what shaped him to the man he'd become and if it was being a vampire or if there was more.

We walked outside into the sunlight and when he was about to leave to go with Aaron who was waiting across the street on the porch of the general store, I touched his arm and he stopped to look at me. "Thank you for all of this."

He nodded and he'd gone a few steps when I called out, "Blake..." When he turned, I smiled. "Be careful."

"You, too."

15

BLAKE

Aaron and I made our way, not on the trail but close to it. I didn't want to draw attention. We stayed close to the tree line and used it for cover. There would come a time when the Fae King knew we were coming for him, but this wasn't that time. Exposing Claire and her plan now would get her killed, and I couldn't have that.

Right now, we'd gather all the information we could and then we'd wait for the time to reveal further plans.

For an hour or so, we stayed out of sight watching the outpost. The elven guard wasn't particularly intimidating and without the others, Aaron and I could've probably taken them out, but should there be more men inside, we wouldn't survive. Claire needed both of us, so we weren't going to risk it.

No matter what happened, I wasn't going to let her down. I was the reason she was here and in danger and involved at all. For a human to be chasing the fae was not only dangerous, but also insanity.

Claire wasn't just any human, surely, but I couldn't imagine a world without her.

She was more. So much more, and I almost ruined... everything. For her. For me. For her uncle. For every human settlement this side of The Rift.

I sure as hell ruined Guthrie's life.

Flashes of turning over a wagon full of women and children to a group of elves who would pick the ones the Fae King would want and dispose of the rest picked at my thoughts. Some days, the images were distant or even absent, but after the run-in with Guthrie, the full-color images kept playing in my mind.

Claire was the voice of the rebellion.

On this side of The Rift, I could sleep. I dreamed. These days, I dreamed of her. I didn't always know for sure it was her. Sometimes I only saw her running away—those were more nightmares

—but I would've recognized the hair, those long golden strands, anywhere.

"You all right?" Aaron Drakeborne rode next to me. Our horses were almost stopped now because I was daydreaming about Claire. Again.

I nodded. "Yeah. Just thinking." Not that I could tell him about it. He wouldn't understand about my Claire. About how I felt.

"About Claire?" He glanced at me, and I didn't like his sudden insight. I didn't like it at all. Felt too personal.

"About keeping her safe from King Theska. He isn't going to be happy that she's whirling up a tornado against him." It was what I should've been thinking about rather than how the sunlight made her hair more golden and her eyes sparkle.

"A tornado would be a nice touch to start a battle."

"Yeah." Too bad we couldn't call on one. The Fae King had never been across The Rift and tornados didn't happen on this side. There were whirlwinds sometimes, but only to force the landscape to renew. To uproot old and allow a new place to grow. Nature on this side of The Rift was very different from nature on the other.

"The Fae King has an army of elves and trolls,

other fae." Aaron wasn't telling me anything I didn't know. "Magic. And besides, I'm not sure he's ever happy with anything. That's how the world got into this predicament in the first place."

I nodded. He was right. The Fae King would kill without conscience, and he really did always seem to be upset with someone or some thing. He'd kill Claire because cutting off the head of the snake would render whatever army she raised without their leader, without the one who inspired their allegiance. Just the same as killing him would deplete the power of the army he raised.

For an hour more we rode and all I could think of was Claire, the danger she was assuming for herself, the fight it would take to destroy this king's reign of terror. I didn't doubt she was up to it, but I had to find a way to keep her safe through it all, to keep her out of the fray.

Drakeborne had sent a call out to all the Riders to meet us at the junction where we'd first come to assemble and work out our plans for delivery of parcels and letters. It was the original office space we used.

I followed him in. Men from all walks of the settlements had come to hear what we had to say, some good intentioned, some not. Some trustworthy, others who could be bought and that was probably what we were going to have to do. Whatever it took to get the help we needed.

At the front of the room, someone had put a long table and I strode to it like I was the man in charge. I wondered what Claire would think if she could see me now. It didn't matter. She wasn't here, and I had plenty to worry about in the moment. She was safe where she was.

Aaron stood beside me with his arms folded. Dorian sat in the front row. He was another Drakeborne—faster, stronger—and we needed all of the Drakebornes we could get. Some of the others—Tom, Joseph, Mark, Dylan, and Jace Ludlow, Elias Roddy, Gabe Santel, Tristan Mccoy, Jack Halloway, Henry Turner—filed into seats in front of the table. Other stood. Still more crowded in until all the Riders cramped inside the building.

If I knew the fae army or the men who would raise the army were all stuffed into one place, I would lock it down and light the match myself. Mercenary or not, a war was a war and there were risks to both sides. I would slash those risks in half before they had time to start if I were the Fae King.

Thankfully, the King didn't know.

Instead, before we could start, one of the elven

patrols rode up out front. There were six of them on horseback and their smell arrived a few moments before they did.

Elves smelled sweet, like berries and wine. Trolls smelled like swamp and manure. I didn't know if the humans could smell it, but we all did, and it created a bit of a commotion.

Five elves and one very pungent troll headed our way and none of us knew what was going on.

The leader of the elves, Rothilion Wranra, was tall. A fighter with a loaded quiver on his back and an arrow in his left hand, he looked every bit the part of someone ready to defend and protect. He had long white-blonde hair, slender fingers, and the body of a man who ran more than he rode. He wore brown leather breeches with silken tassels down the outer leg seams and a white shirt with a brown hat that had a wide brim and a curved crown. But he was no more a cowboy than I was a banker.

Elves were faster than humans, but slower than vampires. His arrow and quiver meant nothing here amongst the Riders. We would be on him before he managed to pull one sharpened weapon from his supply, and I was sure he knew it.

He walked to the front of the room near where I stood and turned to address the men while almost salivating with the anticipation of whatever it was, he wanted to tell us. As safe as we knew we were in the meeting room with him, he knew he was equally safe. He rode in with six, but there would be more, stationing themselves out in the tree line, some out in the open even, and if he'd brought more than the one troll, some would be burrowing underground. If one of us happened to make a move, they would indeed blockade us inside and torch the place.

We all knew the stakes.

"The king of this land hereby decrees that no Rider shall come armed or with designs of battle in his blackened heart." He spoke with a voice that was like a melody, like a sweet song of threatening words.

"There is no king of this land. The king is only ruler of the fae and those too weak to fight him." I was picking a fight without a good reason other than I didn't like his politics. "Are you his errand boy?"

He didn't like being taunted, but was unable to sneer or growl, so he yanked an arrow with one hand and his bow with the other. He aimed the tip at my heart. It was sharpened wood. Well, well, well. King Theska was full of anticipatory measures.

I stared at the arrow, then at the elf holding it. "Go ahead. I'm not your biggest worry."

He threw his head back and laughed. "My biggest worry? I don't worry."

Before he finished the sentence, I was on him because that split second gave me all the time I needed. When he stopped laughing, it was because I had his arrow in my fist against his throat. I could kill him and none of his little friends outside would know. "You're either really tough or really stupid coming in here all alone."

He smiled at me because killing made elven hearts as happy as loving did. "Go ahead, vampire. I'm willing to die for my king. What would you die for?"

I knew the answer, but I was never going to say it. Instead, I pulled the arrow back and smashed the pointed tip in my fist, turned my hand over and blew the dust in his face. "Run along."

"The king will kill you before you can come against him."

I laughed. "He can try." I hadn't survived this long by letting a fae get the better of me. Of course, I also hadn't gone against a Fae King and his army.

The elf took some shoves on his way out, but he walked out. It wasn't until he was outside that he went down, felled by an arrow from one of his men.

Rothilion Wranra's fall from glory pushed the tip

of the arrow out his back, through the long silver tunic near his spine. He hissed a ragged exhale, then breathed his last breath into the clay earth.

Behind him was the man with a carved bow still poised in his left hand, sitting high in the saddle atop his armored horse, but there was no arrow loaded, no indication he was going to take another shot.

Instead, the shooter climbed down from his horse and threw his weapon to the side into the tall grass. He came toward me, and I was ready for anything, to pounce, to jump out of the way, to fight, but I remained standing.

"Blake Rider"—as if my name only now struck him as odd, he cocked his head and started again—"Blake Rider, you have the allegiance of the Elveen of Yelhana. From now until always, we are at your stead."

I wasn't sure what to think. I didn't know if this was limited to the four elves left after Rithilion died or if there were more. But a second later, another elf climbed down from his horse and knelt in front of me. "The Elvene of Daxilim." Then the leader from Ilharna and the one from the Elvene Rojor did the same.

Finally, the troll climbed down, limped toward me because all trolls were born with one leg shorter than the other, and then kneeled on the shorter leg. "The Clan Ekon"—his troll people— "also follows you. We fight when you fight. Sleep when you sleep. Eat when you eat."

I held my arms wide to welcome them all.

The army was building.

16

CLAIRE

By the time the Blake and Aaron returned, I'd made arrangements to meet with the town to talk about joining us against King Theska. We were set up in the church because it was the one place that fit everyone.

Before the meeting started, Blake pulled me to the side. "We have four troops—I don't really know what they're called—of elves that have promised their support and a clan of trolls."

It was good news. Better than I expected, anyway. I'd only expected that the Riders would join our cause and only because they'd agreed to follow

Blake. "How did that happen? I thought you were just going out to watch the outpost?"

"Many of the elves and the trolls have long been under the King Theska's power. They want to be free. Maybe they are finally realizing what's at stake."

A strand of hair blew in my face from the breeze coming through an open window and he reached as if he wanted to push it back, but at the last second, pulled his hand away.

I tucked the curl behind my ear and smiled, my skin hot at the thought of him touching me with such familiarity. *Maybe someday*, I hoped.

My heart pounded. To want him was madness, but I was powerless to stop the need inside me. Maybe this was meant to be, why I'd responded to the ad in the paper, why Blake had been the one to come to take me across The Rift. I couldn't think about it now that we were in this position. As we waited for everyone to come inside, Blake stood next to me, his body close, his eyes piercing.

When they were all inside, men from this town and two others who'd ridden today to get here, I explained that the objective wasn't solely to overtake the Fae King and stop his abuse and plunder of the settlements, but to find those he'd taken, dragged from their homes, or had abducted from either side of The Rift.

"I don't have no family missing, no reason to fight in a war that don't have nothing to do with me." Charlie Potter stood as if to walk out, but two of his neighbors—a Hathaway and a Butler—stopped him.

"Charlie," Butler said, his hand on Charlie's chest. "Your family's been safe, but it's only a matter of time before the king finds one of our towns, one of our kids. His magic grows stronger with every fae under his command and he's breeding them like bunnies. One day it *will* be you. It's like letting a wolf run free among the farms and thinking it's going to leave your sheep alone. One day, it will get your sheep."

That part I didn't know. I would have to ask Blake about the breeding later, but if this logic worked, I wasn't going to contradict it.

Butler was big with shoulders like an ox and a pair of black pants, patched with brown mud at the knees and ankles. His shirt was white once upon a time, but now it was dingy and yellowed. He wasn't the kind of guy a lot of folks would argue with, and Potter stopped trying to leave, but his scowl—deep and unconvinced—remained in place.

The raid was going to take place at nightfall and

more Riders came in the back door as I spoke. "There are women missing from every settlement and my aim is to bring them all home. To stop this terror. I need men who are willing to fight, who can shoot, and who aren't afraid." I shook my head. "*Not afraid* isn't what I mean. I mean, I need men who can face fear and work past it." Fear was fine so long as it wasn't the crippling kind.

I could feel the emotion bouncing around the room and I could see the beginnings of hope. A chill washed over me—one that almost buckled my knees.

I looked out the window, and on a hill not far in the distance, King Theska sat on his mount. I'd never seen him before, but it would've been hard for him to have been anyone else. I just knew it was him. He couldn't see the town, but it still felt close. We would have known if the wards had been breached if the markers had been found. He rode closer, pausing frequently and seeming to listen.

I stared at him for a moment. Tried not to let the panic set in, but he was every bit as impressive as I expected him to be. Tall in his saddle. Regal. The only thing that could've given away the location of the city was the sound of a very angry pegasus trying to escape his corral.

While the King Theska could hear Peggy's

ruckus, he couldn't see him which likely saved the entire town. That was some powerful witch magic. But the king himself had come out on a patrol, which was a risk probably not worthy of the reward.

He looked left then right, then stood in the stirrups of his saddle. I looked at Blake who'd already started toward the side door. He was outside and except for the impending danger, I wished I'd brought Neev.

Instead of harping on that particular mistake, I memorized all the little things about him I could see. The long fingers tipped with stark white nails. The hair. The mannerisms.

I even watched his horse—a white stallion that stamped and stomped and snorted so that a mist blew out its nose. His mane was also snowy white and braided into lots of small braids, but it was the eyes—they glowed red—that told me everything I needed to know. That beautiful beast was under some horrible magic.

Powerful, too, powerful enough to enchant a horse.

After a moment, Peggy quieted, so I assumed Blake had managed to calm him, but the king didn't leave. As far as his eye could see, he would only see landscape, plants, trees. But the sound a pegasus made wouldn't be silenced by ordinary magic. It would need its own cover, a spell to hide him, like we would need because the king would keep guards around here, waiting for one of us to leave or for a Rider to ride in and disappear behind a ward.

I glanced at Crystal who'd taken a seat in the front row waiting for the meeting to be over. She was beside Aaron who'd leaned in and spoke quietly to her so that her face brightened with color.

The king was smart. Smart enough to keep us all captive here until he went away. Fortunately, we were smarter and had a few tricks in our arsenal. Speed. Magic. Fighters of many species. And determination to defeat this bastard who thought it was okay to kidnap and imprison and murder whoever fit his purposes at the moment. Our common goal was more powerful than his greed. I hoped.

17

CLAIRE

After the meeting, we set patrols for the borders of the town near the edges of the wards that protected this place. Crystal strengthened the wards and cast extra protections around Peggy. The one thing the king helped was that he'd scared most of the town into siding with us.

Crystal and I sat with Aaron, Blake, four elven leaders and the lord of a troll clan. We were planning a raid on the fae outpost, still guarded by a family of elves. We'd chosen our sides and they would be given one chance to switch teams. If they continued to fight for the king, then they would be accepting the consequences. It was a sad fact, but the price of war.

The king started this one.

The leader of the Yelhana elves sat at the side of the table with the other elves, the troll sat at one end, I sat at the other and Crystal sat between Blake and Aaron. "We'll leave at first light."

Yelhana's leader nodded. "I've been to the outpost. He drew the building with his finger in the dust on the table. "There is a door here." He pointed to the front of the mark he'd made on the table. "Another back here."

This was a man who spoke with a soft voice and a softer gaze. He was the kind of beautiful that only existed in sunsets and fairy tales, and to be in his company, to see the heartbreak on him, was moving. Even if I didn't have a personal connection to someone–Neev, Peggy–who'd been taken, I would've fought for Yelhana.

I looked at him, laid my hand over his. "Did the king take someone close to you?"

He stared for a second with eyes the same soft teal color as the Atlantic Ocean. Then he nodded and looked down at my hand on his. Next to me, Blake bristled, but for a moment, this wasn't about him. It was the first moment in a long time where he wasn't, at least in part, a thought.

"The woman I love."

I glanced at Blake. "Does he breed fae with elves, too?" I thought it was only humans, but I wasn't completely up to date with all my lore from this world. There could've been a thousand details I didn't know. I was more than sure there were at least a thousand details that I didn't yet know. I wished there were a Rift library where I could check out books that told me all the things I needed to know about this place.

Blake shook his head.

But Yelhana spoke. "No. He's a man who wishes sadness to all others. He collects the happiness of everyone he sees around him, and he feasts on it." Now I'd heard anger that could very well be useful in a fight. A man with a personal reason and the anger to back it up was more lethal than one who was fighting for someone else's cause.

Then the leader of Daxilim nodded. "She's my daughter. Her name is Haera. The Fae King raided, and she was the only woman taken." I wondered if it was because of the king's feelings for Haera or his hatred for the elves. "We need to call his name to the heavens so he will be called to answer for his crimes."

The elf of Daxilim nodded. "Theska. We call for Theska to be judged for his crimes."

Name magic was strong. We were going to war

with a king of magical proportion. Knowing whose name to curse probably wasn't so important, but I was glad to hear the name of the evil king spoken aloud. I wanted the name to become commonplace.

When Blake spoke, his voice was soft, silken, like a purr of promise. A short shiver ran through me, touching every inch of my skin.

"Do we know if Haera is connected to Theska or if he's taken her for another reason?" Blake's eyes darted between the father and the man who loved Haera. I liked the kindness inside of him. It came across in the gentleness of his tone. We needed the answers, but we didn't need to force the pain on them, and that Blake recognized that said something about the man he was. Heaven help me, I liked it.

"Theska lusted after her, but she was already mine, already promised to me." The Yelhana elf looked at me, his eyes dark, his head tilted. "We were to be joined."

"The king offered money, land, riches, even magic." The other elf finished the story. "That's why my people are here to help you. The king took what he wanted without regard to Haera's wishes."

I nodded. "Then let's make a plan and get them all back."

We put our heads down and started. Figured

where to station our arrows and guns. Crystal's magic would shield us going in and out of town. Blake and Aaron, the other Riders would help catch any of the king's fighters who managed to get away.

We waited until sunrise to leave. Because of the risk to Peggy in the forest and with King Theska lurking near, I left him and rode out on a horse that was loaned to me by a farmer in the town.

The morning sky was vibrant, a shade of blue so vivid I almost couldn't stand to look at it directly. I also couldn't look away. I didn't remember the sun and the sky in my own world, but this one, this particular morning, I was never going to forget.

We rode out in small groups so Crystal's magic could provide our shield without draining her and by the time we were in the clearing away from the town and the road narrowed to the outpost, my heart was beating so hard I could feel it in my limbs, my stomach, my bones. The anticipation was another entity on the horse with me.

The outpost was a short, stone and beam building, with bars on the windows and padlocks on the doors. Elves surrounded it and from a tower on top they looked out, watching for any approaching intruder. They could've seen us coming, if not for the magic.

I watched for any elf to show a sign of seeing us, but we rode in and then when we were all assembled, Crystal's magic shroud had to lift so she could use her magic in battle.

Everything went to the wind, and we were deep in battle within moments.

Crystal bombarded the tower with magical blasts, rendering the elves incapacitated in a way that it would take more than magic to come back from. I took out a few of the guards with headshots and Blake ripped open throats and tore out hearts. He was fierce and brutal, but the elves standing guard were fighting hard.

The elves we'd brought along fought valiantly, some even against their kin. For a second, until they won, and the other elves yielded, I watched with admiration. They had all fought well.

I couldn't imagine fighting Uncle Silas, but he'd never worked for the man who'd stolen someone I loved. Couple simple reasons for that—I hadn't loved anyone before, and Silas would never work for evil.

The battle was short, surprisingly, and within minutes, the carnage left behind was steaming on the ground and we'd taken the outpost. I couldn't say that fighting was something I enjoyed but standing up for what was right was something I had to do.

One thing was for sure. The next time I was going into battle—I was going to wear pants like the men. Well, as soon as I could get some made in my size. When fighting for what's right, who cares what I'm wearing?

Blake and Aaron went inside, released the women, led them out. The plan was to take them to safety, but I couldn't stop watching Elwin Yalhana.

When he searched the faces for Haera and didn't find her—if he found her, he didn't go to her, and he certainly didn't look any happier for not finding her—his expression went dark, his shoulders slumped, and he closed his eyes and turned away.

I surveyed the rest of the army on our side. There were cuts and bruises, some abrasions that Crystal zapped away with magic, but otherwise, we'd sustained no losses.

There was a line of women, looking around. I climbed off my horse and led him by the reins over to where they were standing. "We're going to check everyone out and then we'll make sure you all get back to Amberhill."

They were all dirty, clothes torn, fearful. I wanted to soothe them, make it easier for them to forget everything that happened to them since they'd been abducted.

I continued, "If you ever need anything, I live in Nobody, and I'll do whatever I can to help all of you." Or any single one of them.

I pulled the money out of my saddle bag and looked at the Riders. I paid them each what I'd promised, and they helped the women onto horses—their horses—and they left in groups. Despite my exhaustion, I felt like it was a job well done. I wasn't sure why some women were being held at the small outpost though. Maybe it was another waypoint.

Evil didn't have a very good map—at least not one that I could decipher.

When everyone was gone, Blake, Aaron, Crystal, and I searched the compound. There were papers and correspondences and things we would have to look through when we got back to Amberhill. We needed to go soon before the king got wind of what happened here and decided to send troops. It would be surprising if he didn't already know.

Now that we'd sent the fighters away—the elves and trolls went back to their homes and the human women with the Riders—we had to be more careful.

Blake and I walked together with Sunshine and my borrowed horse on the outside. We would ride in a minute, but right now, it was nice to walk. "You did a good thing today, Claire."

"We all did."

He smiled and the world was a bit brighter, and for such an already bright place, that said something. "Claire, you've done more in a year here to upset King Theska's plans than anyone ever before you combined. You're smart and strong, and even if you're not here at the end of all this, you've carved a path and there will be someone who picks up the mantle and continues what you started."

His praise washed through me, warm and sweet, and I reached for his hand, held it in mine for a second. Like someone else was in charge of my body, I moved his hand to my mouth and kissed his knuckles. Then, because I needed something more, I leaned in and kissed his cheek.

I was never so forward before in my life and heat from more than embarrassment flooded my cheeks. It hadn't been more than a brush, barely harder than the touch of a feather, but it was still vibrating through me, still making my heart pound inside my chest.

I walked ahead then swung up into the saddle on my borrowed horse. I couldn't ride on alone because the shroud of magic wouldn't protect me if I rode too far ahead, and Blake rode up beside me, but we didn't talk all the way back to Amberhill.

CLAIRE

It took a full day's ride before we arrived in Tront—the next town on my list—and there was a commotion as soon as we got there. It wasn't Riders or fae or even more elves. It was a covered wagon with *Madame Devina* painted in red on the canvas sitting right at the town gates.

"What's going on?" I looked at Blake who rolled his eyes.

But it was Crystal who answered. "Traveling witchcraft." Her nose wrinkled and her lips sneered. Whoever this Madame Devina was, Blake and Crystal weren't impressed.

I glanced from Crystal to the wagon. "Do you know her?"

She nodded but didn't elaborate.

Blake leaned in and the warmth that seemed to seep into my skin when he so much as breathed in my direction washed into me again. "She's about three hundred years old. A seer witch—one of the strongest magical beings. Be careful touching her."

Crystal rode up beside me. "She's powerful. Senses weakness. So... don't let her see any or she will take advantage. We'll need her help, though. She could be a powerful ally."

It wasn't a warning I was going to take lightly. If they were all this apprehensive, then I would be careful, too. Not only because there was fear deep in my stomach ready to bubble out, but there was an excitement. She was a witch reputed to have great power.

Given all that I'd seen on this side of The Rift, I wanted to know everything about Madame Devina.

We rode down the main street. There was a saloon, an inn, a church, a store, and a grain mill. Same thing I'd seen in every town here. The rider station was manned by a friend of Aaron's who came out to greet him as Aaron hitched his horse in front of the station.

"Hello, old friend. You are a sight!" This Rider was small–maybe a foot or so shorter than Aaron and Blake and a couple inches shorter than me. He tossed his long black hair behind him and then tucked it behind his ears. They slapped hands and held on for a second, and I thought they might've been testing each other's strength, but that wasn't the case. They let go, then hugged. I'd seen this form of male ritual before. Silas had done it with a friend in Boston when they'd met for drinks after twenty years of not meeting for drinks.

When they parted again, Aaron introduced us to his friend who called himself Sam Longshadow. Sam nodded to me. "Devina is waiting for you."

"For me?" Had someone announced our arrival already?

He grinned. "She knew you were coming." For a second, he stared, then he cocked his head and laughed. "One of the other Riders came ahead and said you were going to be coming to town to talk to her."

"Can I freshen up first? Get some dinner and rest, and see her tomorrow? We've had an eventful few days." I looked at the inn, longing for a hot bath and a clean bed. The road between here and the outpost was dusty and long, and my borrowed horse didn't ride nearly as smooth as Peggy. More than once, I'd regretted leaving him in the corral in Amberhill because I had aches where a lady should never ache.

Blake nodded at me. "Claire's right. We should rest and meet her tomorrow."

Sam Longshadow laughed. "Devina doesn't like waiting. She would prefer to meet you now." He held my gaze for an extra second. "I can take you. Your friends can go ahead and check-in at the Inn. You can join them shortly."

I looked at Blake. He was unhappy with the idea of being dismissed, but we were guests in this town, here by the good humor of the mayor, and his humor wasn't likely to last if I put his seer witch in bad humor. Besides, if we needed her help, the last thing we wanted to do was make her unhappy.

From the sound of her and the things they'd told me, she was old, very old. Older than my mind could comprehend. Three hundred years old. That was more time than anything I knew of. Except things I'd studied with Uncle Silas that I couldn't quite believe true. Ancient pyramids. A great wall in China. That an unbreachable city had been breached by a wooden horse.

Sam brought me to a house at the end of the

street. It was small, modest, but tidy with a post in front for horses and a spigot at the side for the well. I walked beside him up the porch steps and into the house. The main room was clean with a long table flanked on each side by benches and a fire burning in the large hearth. A gingham curtain was pulled back on the one open window in the, and it let in just the right amount of light and the scent of lavender and rosemary from flowers and herbs outside.

A woman walked in, all smiles and warmth.

I expected gray hair and wrinkles, but she was anything but. She had hair as black as night, darker even and shiny like silk, not wiry as if tainted by age. She had a bosom that was ample and on display over top of a corset top the same shade as her hair. Her skin was porcelain, also unspotted by time. She was beautiful. Full red lips. Eyes the same amber of a sunset. She looked about thirty.

Madame Devina was the kind of woman who made men weak.

"Come and sit, little one." I didn't get that very often these days–I had turned forty without much fanfare–and though I was told I looked much younger; I didn't approach Devina in looking younger than actual age. I sat across from her on the bench closest to me then slid to the middle of the table where I could see her around a milk pitcher. She hadn't sat yet, but she nodded to me when I did. "We'll head to the town hall in a moment."

I nodded. "I'm so pleased to meet you, Madame Devina. My name is Claire Lowell."

Her smile was peaceful, serene, and genuine. "Yes, Claire Lowell. Little wolf. No one thought to warn you that I look like this?" She made a sweeping gesture with her arm then stood in a pose, her umbrella pointed at the floor, hip cocked.

The gingham curtains flapped in the stiff breeze that suddenly came in through the open window. She closed her eyes and smiled.

"No. Crystal and Blake didn't mention anything about your appearance."

She straightened and walked to the table. "How is Mr. Rider?" This smile was more familiar, and my stomach tightened. I didn't want to believe it was jealousy, but it couldn't have been anything else.

"He's well." Too well for my own good.

"He brought you to me because you wish to wage a war, and you believe you need help."

A war. Yes, I did. "King Theska…"

"Is powerful, but you, Claire Little Wolf, are more so. You have the power to defeat him." This time, she tilted her head and nodded. I wanted to believe her, to believe in what she said, but I found it difficult, given all that I knew about him.

"You really think I can defeat him?" I hoped I didn't sound like I was patronizing her. I folded my hands in my lap. I wasn't sure how to act around such a powerful witch, and for the first time in a long time, I was off kilter and unsure of myself.

Devina took a second, looked at me, eyes narrowed, as if she were taking the measure of the kind of woman, I was by simply looking at me. "You've found information at the outpost that will be of use to you." She smiled. "And I'm prepared to help you, if you need me."

"Why? Why would you want to put yourself at risk?" I leaned forward. "I'd love to have your help, of course. But I didn't come to Tront expecting it."

There had to be a reason this woman would be willing to leave her nice safe, warded town. Like the elves and the trolls, she was the kind of woman who wouldn't join unless she had a stake, something to gain if we won or something to lose if we didn't. I wasn't suspicious that she had a secret and terrible reason, but I did wonder why.

"I've seen what you will do next and it's going to have an impact on the king. A great impact on him and his forces."

I wondered for a second if she happened to know what that next move of mine would be, but I didn't ask. For whatever reason, I wanted to look like I knew what I was doing. Maybe it was because of that smile she'd worn when she mentioned Blake. The reason didn't really matter as much as the way I handled it from here on, I guess, but she made me really want to be the person she thought I was.

The self-doubt inside of me was strong, though. "Can I do it? Can I make a difference?" I shook my head because this war had to happen whether this—the good side—won or not. The king couldn't proceed unchecked with his kidnapping and breeding plots. He was ruining the world. And now that I knew what he'd done to the dragons, there was no turning back.

"Once The Rift is sealed, you'll have an even greater impact than you can imagine."

"It can be sealed?"

"Yes." Her eyes widened. "You didn't know?"

"No." I shook my head. "No, I didn't know." It seemed like information one of the people who'd lived on this side would've told me at some point. "Is there even magic that will seal The Rift?"

Devina nodded and patted down her skirt.

"There is magic that will seal it. The good news is…" As if she knew I needed some. "It's a single spell."

Well, that helped. Restored my hope, anyway.

"If you have that magic, why have you never used it?" It would've saved lives, so many humans would have made it to their actual destination. Of course, I wouldn't have met Blake or owned the Bunny… and I would've still been in Boston.

She went back to full serenity—smile, posture, even the way she held her hands flat against the table. "*I* don't have that magic." The smile lingered. "But I know where to get it."

"Oh." I was as eloquent as ever.

"As for taking the war to the Fae King, I saw that I had to wait for you." Her pause was short. "And I've waited years for you to come to me, Claire Little Wolf."

It wasn't that she was blaming me. Her tone would've been sharper—as mine had neared when I asked about her magic.

"What did you mean when you said you saw what I had to do next?" I was good at reading people, even magic ones, and there was something she wasn't saying, something she knew that I needed to know before I could proceed. The problem was, I didn't think she was going to tell me.

She spoke in mysteries, and I wasn't sure if it was because she knew things and didn't like to tell people or if it was because she didn't know things and she liked people to think she knew. Or if it was a bit of both.

"You did well freeing the captives, but now, you must go after their transport." If I looked confused, it was because I was confused.

"Do fae not travel by horse and by magic?" They had so far as I'd seen.

"Some do. Others travel by great winged beasts. Dragons at one time. Until the revolt. Then they started using the pegasusi." She sighed. "You will go to their breeding and training facility. I'll send a few of my men with you."

"I have plenty of Riders." Now, I didn't quite trust her. Because I was right. She wanted something.

"If you survive, I will tell you about the magic to seal The Rift and where to find it."

Now, all I had to do was figure out what she was going to ask for in return.

19

CLAIRE

Something about Tront was off. It took me until we were about to leave to figure it out. Maybe because I was still shaken from my meeting with Devina and her edict that I take her men and go disrupt the travel of the fae when all I wanted to do was bulldoze my way into the town they lived in and find King Theska. Save all the captive people and animals. Bring order and freedom back.

But as I glanced at the people of Tront, the differences—ears with sharp points, flaxen hair that looked like silk, silver eyes, silly smirks that never seemed to fade—stood out to me and panic burned in my belly. Everywhere I looked, I saw a dwarf or an elf or a troll. Then I saw a fae. Then another. And another.

I glanced at Blake who was pulling the girth strap tight around Sunshine's belly, and he looked at me. "Claire?" He put his hand on my shoulder. "Claire? What's wrong?"

My breath stuttered and I couldn't catch it. My heart pounded like it would explode.

"It's all right, Claire. You're safe." I didn't know what he could see in my face, but there was something. "Just breathe." He put his hand on my other shoulder, forced me to look into his eyes which made my heart beat harder, but my breathing came easier. "Good."

"Look around. Can you see fae here or am I going crazy?" I searched his face for a response.

I watched him survey the place and I knew the exact moment he saw what I did. His lips parted and he blinked, widened his eyes, then blinked them closed and open again. "I didn't notice." but now that he had, his expression resumed normal business. "There are towns, this one, I suppose, that are shelters for elves who have escaped the king, or are in hiding, trolls who don't want to be forced into his service, and even lower fae who are sympathetic to humans but pose no threat to the king or anyone else."

I didn't know if that meant their magic had been drained or if there was some other reason, but any of these species posed a threat simply by the fact that humans were powerless against them.

It astounded me, yet again, that there were so many examples of things I didn't know and that I didn't know existed here. Maybe I rushed things, didn't take the time to study my surroundings and this place.

But Devina, a woman who could see the future, supposedly, had not twenty-four hours ago, told me that I was right where I was supposed to be.

"All these people are okay to be here?" My voice wavered and I hated the weakness. "It seems like a perfect set-up for a trap."

"Yes. It's safe. You're safe."

I didn't want to point out that everyone in this town who wasn't human could benefit from the king's generosity in repayment for turning us in. I kept it to myself, and I would, for now. But the first Rider I saw that looked to be any kind of threat and I was going to handle it my way–guns blazing, questions later.

Devina's three Riders were mostly silent during the three days it took to get to our destination—or near it enough we should be able to observe the facility before we busted in disrupted the breeding and training.

It could've been that the king was cocky or so unchallenged during his reign that he wasn't worried about anyone trying to overthrow him, but it seemed to me as we rode up that maybe we were about to be overpowered. Even after all the planning with Devina and the mayor of her city. Even after we'd been introduced to the men she'd sent to surveil the training facility. Even after... everything.

Even the air felt uneasy.

I dismounted next to Blake. He'd ridden beside me most of the way to where we decided to make camp–a rocky and shaded area near enough to the facility that we could see the comings and goings–not that there were many–but far enough the pegasusi wouldn't smell the horses and give up our location.

"We should make camp here tonight. Go in before dawn. When we're rested." Blake's voice was soft, and he was standing close enough I could see the golden flecks in his deep brown eyes, and I could feel his warm breath on my skin.

I nodded because I couldn't speak. Not with him so near. Not without fear of blurting out that I wanted him, and that I couldn't stop thinking about him, and that I'd spent the last few hours of a very long ride wishing for a future I didn't know was possible.

Instead, I breathed out slowly and nodded, smiled just a little bit because his lips parted and he looked down at me, tilted his head to the side. Maybe he wanted this too, at least some of it. Maybe that was enough for now.

"Do you want me to help you with your tent?" He'd never asked me before. I assumed that was because he knew I didn't need his help, and I wondered for just a second if I should play coy now, be the damsel, but I shook the thought off.

"Thank you though." Because I couldn't let the moment pass without making sure there was another soon, I smiled up at him. "Maybe we could... um..." What? Stare up at the stars? Sit in the moonlight and gaze at one another? None of the other things I wanted to do with and to him sounded appropriate for a woman to say to a man, even now. "Do some planning in a little while?" I was out of my league.

Those thoughts flitted through my head over and over again as I pitched the tent, unrolled my bedding and sat for a moment, trying to pull myself together until a shadow the size of one very delectable vampire fell over my tent. "Claire?"

His voice wasn't much more than a hushed whisper, but I heard it and it went straight to my heart. I loved the way he said my name. The way his eyes changed when he spoke to me, the way...

Gosh darn it, of all the times to realize my feelings might be spinning out of control, this was a bad one.

But I opened the flap of the tent and invited him in. He ducked inside and sat at the end of my bed roll. I was near the middle. I could've touched him without reaching far at all. His eyes were a soft caramel color in the lantern light. The glow cast shadows on his face and put color into his cheeks that wasn't normally there.

I could've stared at him all night and been happy to do it when I should've been all business, when I should've been watching the training facility, figuring out our next moves after we derailed this place, but all I could do was stare.

"Claire." It wasn't a question or a plea or like he was about to make a request. It was the sweetest whisper I'd ever heard. I wanted to touch him. I had urges beyond what would normally be acceptable, had ideas of things I wanted to try. I wanted to know all about him.

"Have you eaten lately?" I spoke the words quietly, but firmly. I was pretty sure I knew the answer.

At the words, his eyes flared, and he shifted so he was an inch or so closer. He knew what I was offering.

"I'm all right."

"I know this wasn't the plan for you and we should already be back at home, but…" I closed my eyes. "I can't trust you to be the guy who is helping me plot and plan and execute if you're crazy with hunger." I lifted my sleeve. "Please, Blake." My voice was breathy, soft with need.

He closed his eyes for the space of a second, the war inside of him raging on his face. His expressions changed as what he wanted and what he needed battled for space.

He took my arm in his hands like I'd handed him something precious. He stared for a second, then pressed his lips against my skin. *Oh God.* They were as silky as I remembered, as full and perfect.

There was a pinch of pain then my body

warmed, burned, and the fingers of the hand he wasn't holding tangled in his hair as my head fell back. *Oh God.* There was nothing like this feeling. It was desire and want and need twisted into an emotion so strong I couldn't breathe.

I couldn't speak around it. I whimpered when no other sound would come.

Lust swirled in my belly. Hunger churned inside of me. Need. Desperation. I moved closer, chest heaving as he lifted his head. And I kissed him with all the pent-up desires of a woman who'd never known a passion like this one.

He tilted his head and deepened the kiss, his tongue sliding against mine, his hand cupping my face, his thumb stroking my cheek. I didn't want it to ever end.

Too soon, it did. It could've gone on forever and still ended too soon for me. But I smiled when he pulled back, his hand still on my face, mine still curled in his hair. I pulled away and started unbuttoning my blouse, one tiny button at a time.

He watched for the smallest time possible, then laid his hand over mine. "Claire." This time there was a finality to his voice.

Dammit. There was no reason. We were adults.

I leaned in again and this time he moved back. It hurt in places I didn't know I could hurt.

"Oh, Claire." His voice was soft, a caress I didn't need. "I want to be with you." He brushed the hair back off my face. "I want to, but when that happens, I want it to be because you want it, not because of bloodlust."

Bloodlust. Such an interesting word.

He stood and walked out, and I fell back on my bedroll. This was more than bloodlust. This was honest. I wanted him when I wasn't reeling from the feel of his mouth against my skin. I wanted him when I woke and when I fell asleep at night, when I walked around during the day planning how to dethrone the Fae King. Every minute of every day the desire was there.

I looked down at my wrist. The bite mark had already healed, but when I closed my eyes, I could still feel his fingers, holding my arm like it was the most delicate flower.

It wasn't just about all this. It was the kindness in him. The man himself.

It took about five minutes before the realization hit me. Before I recognized this feeling for what it was.

I might just love him.

20

BLAKE

That woman was more than any other I'd ever met. And I'd met my share. She was all the goodness that was left in people, in the entire world. And I wanted her so bad I almost couldn't stop myself. Not the feeding. That was a fullness inside of me. But Claire was an ache. Not Claire herself, but the need. Need to hold her, to feel the warmth of her body on mine.

This time, when I fed on her, it wasn't like the last. This time, because I wasn't focused on dying, I could focus on her. Feel her emotion. It was intoxicating. The way liquor used to be.

Claire wasn't the kind of woman who would let passion sidetrack her goals. She wanted to see this through and a dalliance with me wouldn't fit into her plans. She would fight her attraction and I couldn't be the thing that came between her and what she had to do.

Morning came and we were on foot now. I knew from how Peggy reacted to Sunshine that the pegasusi in this building would react to the smell of the horses we rode, so we had to leave them behind. There was no way around it.

Aaron had spent the night watching the facility. He crouched between me and Claire where we waited for the "There aren't many soldiers here."

It made sense since they only trained animals here that the fae wouldn't believe that anyone would attack the place.

That's what we hoped.

When we were still at Tront with Devina and she'd already told Claire we were going to disrupt the training facility, she'd sent one of the Riders back for Peggy. The pegasus had only just arrived and the Rider, frustrated by the contrariness of the beast left for the town on the horse she'd ridden in.

I nudged her. "Maybe we should use Peggy and you could shoot from the air."

Crystal, on her other side, nodded. "It's a good idea. I can cloak you with magic until you're ready."

I liked having Crystal with us. She'd been so helpful with so many things. Not just with the magic.

Mostly I wanted Claire in the air, so she wasn't so exposed, so in danger.

"No. I don't want to be up there. I want to be here with everyone else." By not saying it, Claire wasn't hiding her desire. She wanted to be in the thick of the battle. She wanted to fight. I couldn't deny her. Without her, none of this would be going on. There would be no hope for those captured and held by the king. To be honest, I didn't know if they knew we were trying to save them, if they knew we were coming, but I hoped so.

The facility was quiet—no sign of unusual activity or anything amiss. Not yet. It looked like what would be an ordinary day at a training facility. At least what I would expect. A few guards stood around in a group talking and laughing and not really doing much guarding. A bit farther away, some people, maybe elves, led a couple of pegasusi to a feeding trough or maybe a watering trough.

"Are you ready?" Claire looked around Aaron at me.

"Yes." We stood almost in unison. Opened fire. Warning shots first, aimed away from the facility.

Enough to sound like a brigade of soldiers was upon them. Of the ten or so elves guarding, one fired back with an arrow and Claire shot him in the hand. She was careful not to kill unless the death was necessary.

The initial assault took only seconds, less than a minute, certainly. The slaves who were taken by the king and forced here to train the pegasusi–elves who could speak to animals like Neev–were on the ground, hands over their ears. "Please! Please don't kill us."

Various voices made the same request, some teary, some merely fearful.

Claire was inside with Crystal opening the pens that housed each pegasus. The creatures ran out past us and into the open yard. Some took flight. Some stayed on the ground, circling and testing their freedom. Hoofbeats echoed against the walls and an occasional whinny reverberated.

I didn't know exactly if Peggy could understand Claire, but she came out and called him over. "Talk to them. Tell them that if they fight with us against the Fae King, I will promise that they will never have to fight again for their freedom." But like he understood her words, he went to the sky, hovered, seemed to be communicating with howls and shrieks, snorts, and neighs.

More and more beasts took to the air, until the sky was filled with pegasusi of all colors. Peggy seemed to talk to each one, and others spread the word as they hovered and pranced about on the wind.

Not that I didn't like having the winged horses with us, but I didn't trust them. I didn't like that they were so powerful. Prior to meeting Peggy, I'd never met one I liked. Even though I suspected that Peggy's sudden interest in nuzzling my hand and nuzzling my face were only an attempt to get close to Sunshine. It was something to discuss with Claire, another commonality, but I hadn't done it yet because it seemed trivial in the grand scheme of the things she had on her mind.

I watched, with my head tilted up, as Peggy continued to speak to the other animals. My stomach though, my gut feeling, told me there was something off, not right about this and how easy it had been. Then, another pegasus, a male, circled Peggy for a second before he leapt, attacking with bats of wings and hoof kicks that should've sent Peggy careening toward the ground. But he stayed aloft, fighting, giving as well as he took.

But it was that moment, that spectacle above us that caused my focus on my own surroundings to waver. A door in the ground opened and four soldiers dressed in the Fae King's uniform crawled out.

"Claire!" I don't know how I screamed, or if it was even me.

The sound of the first shot echoed through my head and I ran, used every special bit of speed I had to get between Claire and the bullet.

The thing about being shot was the intense hot pain that seared a path through skin and muscle and bone. Even as quickly as I could heal, there was pain in being shot, in having a bullet rip through my body and for her, I took seven more shots before she had picked off the last guard. They were on the ground in a neat row, the same as they had been standing as they came out of the ground, and now each had a bloody hole in the center of his forehead.

As I fell to my knees–healing from this many gunshot wounds would take time even for me—I managed to look back over my shoulder and saw the tears glinting in Claire's eyes before I passed out in the dirt.

21

CLAIRE

When things calmed down, and after Blake regained consciousness, stood and shook off the dust from falling, I breathed softly, slowly, hoping the panic in my heart would abate. I knew he was practically invincible, but this was the second time he'd taken shots to save my life. It was getting to be a habit and I had to figure out a way to not get shot at anymore. Watching him fall like that, not knowing if this would be the time he died from the injuries was almost more than my heart could take.

"Ready?" He motioned to the opened bunker door in the ground the soldiers had climbed out of. When I looked inside, I saw shelves made of wood and metal. I climbed down the ladder in front of the bunker then stood up in the underground hole. The bunker was an open pit with earthen walls lined with shelves full of guns. Rifles. Shotguns. Pistols. Boxes and rolls of ammunition. Extra parts. So many guns.

This was a weapons storage depot. Hidden in the middle of a simple training facility. Brilliant. If the soldiers would've stayed put underground until we freed the animals and left, it would've gone unfound. They had made a costly mistake.

I picked through the shelves, looking through the boxes of ammo. We'd be able to use it all. What an amazing find. Most of the guns were newer—much newer than most of the weapons we had.

At the end of one of the shelves was a small door with a cut out about halfway up.

I glanced at Blake who walked in front of me. If there was another soldier inside, he didn't want me to be hurt, and despite his healing injuries, he still insisted on protecting me. I nodded as he yanked the handle and the door pulled back.

He looked inside. "Claire."

I moved around him and peeked inside, careful not to hit my head on the dusty wooden frame of the door. Inside, backed against the wall, was a young woman whose face was brown with dirt, whose hands were raw, nails broken from where she'd been trying to dig her way out.

"Hi. Are you okay?"

She hugged her knees and nodded. Her torn dress was so tattered I could barely recognize it was a dress and not a nightgown.

"What's your name?"

"Mara." Her voice was meek, small.

She was younger than I thought, maybe a teenager, with long scraggly hair and a frame thinned by a lack of food.

"You're safe now. Do you want to leave? I can help you out of here."

"Yes." She nodded then scooted toward me.

I held my arms out to her.

She stopped, recoiling. "Are you Claire?"

I paused. "Y-yes. My name is Claire. Why?"

"I dreamed you rescued me." She looked up at me with big blue eyes. "You had shorter hair."

I noticed then that she was fae. I stepped back, bumping into Blake. He put a hand on my shoulder.

"It's okay. She's not a risk," he whispered. "I can feel that she's okay."

I stared at him a moment. He'd not given much indication before that he could read people by feeling anything. But I trusted him. I turned to Mara.

"I rescued you?" I tried to smile. In truth I felt sadness for the child, but I had to admit I was nervous about her being fae. I'd not had good luck with the Fae here on this side of the Rift.

"Yes," she stood and walked toward me, taking my hand as she got close. "You and a dragon rescued me and saved the world."

I looked at Blake and he shrugged.

"Well, I guess I rescued you, but I don't have a dragon. Maybe this vampire will have to do." I pointed to Blake.

Mara smiled.

I would have to talk more with Mara and find out what else she had seen in her dreams, but for now, she needed a good meal, a bath, and a soft bed to rest.

I looked at all the elves we'd freed. So many looked like Neev or similar to him. If they were all as nice, then these kids were going to be a joy.

"I won't hurt you," I said when I reached to help one to his feet. "My name is Claire Lowell. I only need information." No one stepped forward. "I promise you won't be hurt." I looked at the youngest one and he reminded me of Neev. "Is it..." I didn't know how to ask the question in a gentle way, so I just asked. "Can you speak to animals?"

The young one nodded at me but didn't speak.

"I rescued a boy named Neev from the Fae King's captivity. Do you know him?" I looked at each of them as they nodded.

"Neev is my friend. I'm Vind." The young one smiled at me. "Thank you for saving him. And us."

I smiled back. "Neev has the gift that you all have. Do all elves have it?" That wouldn't make sense.

The young one shook his head. He was quite handsome, as most elves were. His smile made him look even younger. "No. Not all of us can communicate with them."

"But the ones who can he turns to slaves?" I looked at them. It wasn't a coincidence that they all had the gift, and they were all enslaved.

The young one nodded again. "There isn't a formula for who he takes, but once he finds one of us or is told of one of us, we're taken. He uses some sort of mind manipulation to control the fae and some of the other species." He smiled just a little bit. "The king can't control our minds."

Obviously or they wouldn't be speaking to me now.

This entire journey had been one mind-shattering discovery after another.

I looked at the elves still sitting on the ground. "Would you like to travel with our group back to the town where I live? Or you can go your own way. Or right now, we have Riders going back to a town that is a safe haven for all. Whether you're elven or troll, fae or human."

They huddled and their low voices made me smile. "We would like to go back to the safe haven. For now, at least. We need to rest and get strong."

I nodded, shook hands with each of them. "Be very safe." It was a wish for them and a warning. There were dangers here to them that they needed to be aware of.

I walked them over to Devina's Riders and handed them a note I had quickly scrawled to thank her for her kindness and for the Riders she'd sent with us. I also added that I would be in touch. She was an ally now and we would need to communicate. Mara and a few other fae were also going to go back to Tront. I'd asked Devina to take care of Mara but I planned to talk to her soon about the girl—and find out how she knew about me.

Oh, did I have a lot of questions for her.

As I walked back to where Blake stood with Crystal and Aaron, the horses were loaded with our belongings and a couple of the pegasusi were loaded down with the weaponry we'd confiscated.

Blake limped toward Sunshine, and I glanced at Crystal. "I did what I could, but he took a lot of bullets. He said he just fed, but without fresh blood, it's going to be a minute before he can completely heal."

I had my first worry-free moment in a very long while. And I looked at Blake, wanting what I always wanted now, to be near him. To touch him. To feel his mouth pressed against mine. To let him know that I wanted this.

There was no hesitation in my step when I walked up to him and pulled him down for a kiss so steeped with passion that it rocketed through me, stark and powerful. Dear heaven, I wanted this man.

When we parted, I glanced over his shoulder at Crystal and Aaron. He had wide eyes, mouth slightly open, but her slight smirk said she was a bit less surprised than Aaron.

I smiled at him. "I didn't want you to misunderstand this time. I kissed you because I wanted to without the bloodlust. So don't blame that." When I held out my arm, he grinned.

"Understood." Then he fed. Not as much as last night, but enough the lust slinged into my blood and my eyelids fluttered closed. It was a reaction I couldn't control. Neither could I control my mind and it was all on him, his mouth, his hands, his body and how I wanted him to use them.

But when he finished, I lowered my sleeve and walked back to Peggy. Crystal came to stand beside me. She touched my shoulder, and I could feel a glow come over me, and the passion abated.

"Thank you," I whispered. She deserved more but shook her head and held up her hand.

She laughed a little. "You don't have to thank me. For goodness sake, just give me a job if I ever come looking for one."

I nodded and we walked over to where the pegasusi all seemed to be waiting for me.

22

CLAIRE

The trip back to Nobody was long and tedious, especially since we had so many extra beasts to keep flying in the right direction. Some of them—about seven, actually—simply didn't want to walk, so Blake handled the ones on hoof, and I tried to corral the ones on wing.

To say it wasn't easy was laughable. It was nigh impossible.

There were a few who had decided to go their own way. They were older, flew less swiftly than the ones with us now. As we made our way back to Nobody the thoughts that had given me reprieve long enough to kiss Blake were back. We still had other towns to visit, other allies to gain, and I didn't know how much time we had before the Fae King took advantage and attacked us while we were scattered. I was sure he would be upset at all the people we had freed and all the places we had destroyed.

Not for the first time, as I chased down another wayward pegasus, one carrying the weaponry, I wished I'd brough Neev along or that one of the other elves with animal communication powers had decided to come along with us. Their particular gifts would've made this trip home much easier.

I looked down at Blake. He'd told me as we left the facility that I was going to be a grandmother.

Apparently, Sunshine had succumbed to Peggy's charms and was going to have his colt.

I wasn't sure if I wanted to know how that had happened. Well, I knew how those things happened, but I meant, how he'd talked her into it since she was usually so annoyed with him.

On the way back to Nobody, when we camped at night, we unloaded the weapons from the pegasusi carrying them. If they needed to fly, I didn't want them possibly carrying off the king's wares.

I couldn't coax Blake into my tent, though. No matter how hard I tried.

When we sat under the stars, I laced my fingers

with his and smiled. "Blake, I want to be with you." I thought saying the words would be enough.

"Not here. Not like this." His words were soft, but a rejection anyway and the near whisper quality wasn't enough to ease the pain they inspired.

I tried again on the second night. "You could sleep in my tent tonight." I was past being coy. I was aching with need and with want and only he could make it better.

He tucked my hair behind my ear, and I leaned my head back against the trunk of a tree I was standing beneath. We'd been sitting together enjoying the sounds of silence that weren't so silent. There'd been night animals burrowing, owls hooting, the pegasusi snorting, the horses nickering. Crystal and Arron laughed in the distance, softer, but still breaking the silence.

His gaze pointed at mine. "I would like that, so much." For a second I had hope. "But I want you properly. In a bed. Cherished."

"A bed of grass?" A girl could try.

He smiled.

By the time we rode into town, all I wanted a hot soak in a magic bath. If there was something to be said about this side of The Rift, it had to be those hot soaks.

And I wanted to get to the saloon where Uncle Silas would be with Neev if they weren't at the house. And I hoped they weren't at the house.

Instead of a long soak followed by a night's sleep not complicated by the sounds of night, the bath was short and instead of my pillow and blanket, I went to the Dusty Bunny where I hoped my uncle wasn't teaching Neev everything he knew.

The house was too quiet for me to be able to sleep, anyway.

I walked into the saloon, smiled at customers old and new. And I saw them immediately. Uncle Silas. The sweet elven boy I'd left with him who'd sworn he was sixteen but looked about twelve.

He tipped back a shot of amber liquid—bourbon and probably the good stuff, knowing Silas—and slammed his fan of cards onto the table, collected the pot and smiled. "Hell yeah, baby." His voice was still that of a boy even with the swear word and the whiskey glass in front of him.

Silas poured him another drink.

I glanced at Cherry, and she shrugged. It was a

"what can you do" situation and I pulled closer the shot of whiskey she'd poured for me without my asking. I drank, enjoyed the burn of it in my throat for a second before I swallowed it, then sat the glass upside down on the bar. This was my life now. What a life it was.

•

23

BLAKE

We'd been back for several days and resisting Claire was hard, harder than it had ever been before. She was as alluring as any woman I'd ever met. Honestly, more so.

I respected her too much to mess things up though.

I was on a pegasus because Sunshine and Peggy had done made a baby and she was resistant to my saddle now. Threatened me with those eyes of her when I even brought the thing into her paddock. She wasn't having it, so I was on this wild beast of a winged horse. They were hard to control, stronger than any horse. I wasn't enjoying my time on patrol.

Neev had called him FireWind and once he understood that I wouldn't hurt him, and that I called him by his name instead of anything less familiar, I seemed to garner his respect. He followed the commands anyway.

With still no sign of Clayton and the mad king on the loose, I couldn't stop the nerves in my gut. I flew the border around the wards. It was the fastest way to patrol and made the most sense. Claire was inside the wards, and I needed to make sure she stayed safe. Without her, this all failed.

The pegasus soared and I patted his neck. His auburn coat shined in the sun, and I wondered if I was ever going to be able to go back to simply riding a horse. Not that I would abandon Sunshine, but this feeling of flying was addictive, and I could understand why Claire loved Peggy so much.

I made one last sweep around the border, then landed FireWind near the stream at the border of town. A twig snapped. A flight of birds flew out of the tree line. My senses heightened. This wasn't an animal.

A second before the first pure silver round tore into my skin, I saw him.

Clayton.

He stepped out, closer, his hands still clenching

the gun. "What's the matter, Blake? Your little blood bag isn't here to save you this time?" I was on the ground when he shot me again and my body jerked, curled. "You aren't anything without her, are you? Nothing."

My head ached. My guts churned. "What do you... How..."

"How did I get the drop on such an accomplished piece of work like you?" He was mocking me. Even as the world started to fade, I could hear it over the pounding in my ears. He pulled a pendant out of his shirt. "Fae magic, son." He was too proud, too arrogant to be lying. "I stole it, used it to cloak myself in blackness when they were going to torture me." He paused, lit a cigarette, and laughed. "It's funny what you can see when you're on that side." he looked down at the pendant. "If you weren't the bastard you are, I might've let you try it."

The pain dulled and I knew what that meant. These were silver bullets—I felt that burn immediately—and I was going to die. Nothing I could do now.

He pulled out a paper and used the blood pooling around me to write a note. Then he took the knife from my belt and used it to stab the note into the pegasus who yelped and cried in pain, curled to its knees, but didn't move toward Clayton.

It had to be the fae magic still protecting him.

Clayton jerked me up and bound my hands even as my knees collapsed and I nearly fell, but he yanked me to my feet once more. "That should make your little girlfriend come running to save you. Or should I say, *try* to save you."

He marched me to the tree line as I stumbled and fell, then forced me onto a horse that had also been hidden. Or I hadn't noticed. What had made me so blind to the danger? Clayton hadn't ever been that smart, at least not that I realized. Maybe I hadn't given him enough credit.

No telling what this bastard planned do. One thing was for sure. If he hurt Claire, I would hunt him to death and beyond. He'd rue the day, no, the very moment he even thought about hurting her.

I swore it.

EPILOGUE

CLAIRE

I sat in the office, my list of allies in front of me, growing ever longer as I compiled more names to add. We had the elves and the trolls clan, Devina and the entire town of Bront, the Riders, some of the lower fae from Amberhill.

But I was restless. I couldn't just sit in the office and wait for word. I walked out into the saloon and smiled at Cherry and Max and some of the others who were playing poker and drinking at tables. I wanted to see how Silas was adjusting, too, so I walked to his table and stood at the edge. He was playing cards with Hughes and a Donough.

I hadn't seen Blake in a while. Probably an entire

day and then it wasn't much more than a wave as he headed out on yet another patrol. It wasn't unusual that I hadn't seen him. He had duties with the Riders and was sometimes gone for days, but if he'd left, he would've mentioned it.

Maybe even kissed me goodbye like a proper suitor.

We were making small steps in the progress of our relationship, if one could even call it that. And I was still a bit reluctant to even talk about it. Partly because I wasn't sure how Uncle Silas would react to my having someone in my life, even though he liked Blake, had even said Blake impressed him.

Silas was one observant man. Details seldom found a way past his notice, so I was sure he knew about me and Blake. Almost positive, even. Soon, we would have to talk about it, but now, when he was three aces into a hand of stud wasn't the time.

Maybe I was restless because I'd hoped being back would give me and Blake some time together to work on us. Maybe we could even figure out what was going on between us and if it was just the connection of me letting him feed off my blood or if it was more. I was sure it was much more, but I didn't know how he felt. Or maybe I was scared to trust that it was more.

My stomach tightened and a wave of apprehension came over me. I didn't know why. Things at the Bunny were fine. Neev was sitting at the bar reading a Penny Dreadful Silas had given him and taught him to read while I was gone.

I'd been out to see Peggy and the horses earlier. Everyone seemed to be getting along and the new pegasusi were all in their own corral, free to go, free to stay—whatever they wanted. Neev had told them of the dangers of leaving and the risks of being captured by the fae, and that it was their choice whether to head out on their own or stay for a while under our care. Only one had gone after we returned.

But something in the air wasn't right. My belly said so. "You all right, boss lady?" Cherry asked in her slow, sweet southern drawl.

"Yeah. I think so." But I wasn't, and we both knew it. She smiled and handed me a glass of ale. It would do for now.

Before I took a single swallow, the saloon doors burst open, and Aaron came running inside.

He was long and lean, eyes glowing with something I didn't think was anger. His step was too quick for anger, to light. He was the type of man who let his rage simmer into something that burned hotter than fire and heavier.

This wasn't that.

"Aaron?"

He nodded. "I was on patrol and just outside the barrier, I smelled blood." He closed his mouth for a second and took a long inhale. "Come look." He motioned me to follow.

I followed him outside to the pegasus that Blake had started riding while Sunshine was carrying her foal.

"I found this one on the ground beside a pool of blood." He closed his eyes then opened them to look at me. "Vampire blood." He shook his head. "I walked him back as quickly as we could. But he had this stabbed into his neck."

He handed me the note.

If you want to see Blake again, you will come alone, and bring my guns.

ABOUT KERRY ADRIENNE

USA Today bestselling author Kerry Adrienne loves history, science, music, and art. She's a mom to more cats than children and she loves live music, traveling, and staying up all night. Because...vampires. She writes romance (paranormal, m/m, historical, time travel, and more), science fiction, and fantasy. In addition to writing books, she's also a college instructor, artist, costumer, editor, and bad guitar player.

Find out more about Kerry Adrienne here:

Website: https://kerryadrienne.com/

Facebook: https://www.facebook.com/authorkerryadrienne

Twitter: @kerryadrienne

TikTok: https://vm.tiktok.com/ZM8wPhnjx/

Please sign up for her newsletter here:

https://www.subscribepage.com/kerryadrienne

Monthly contests and news... (and cats! Lots of cats!)

ABOUT L.A. BORUFF

USA Today Bestselling Author L.A. (Lainie) Boruff lives in East Tennessee with her husband, three children, and an ever growing number of cats. She loves reading, watching TV, and procrastinating by browsing Facebook. L.A. is passions include vampires, food, and listening to heavy metal music. She once won a Harry Potter trivia contest based on the books and lost one based on the movies. She has two bands on her bucket list that she still hasn't seen: AC/DC and Alice Cooper. Feel free to send tickets.

ALSO BY KERRY ADRIENNE

The Orb of Oriste:

Raven's Game

Dragon Myst (coming soon)

Dragon Storm (coming soon)

Dragon Ember (coming soon)

Shifter Wars:

Waking the Bear

Pursuing the Bear

Taming the Lion

Claiming His Lioness

DSD (with Lia Davis):

Dragon Undercover

Snowed Undercover

Captain Undercover (coming soon)

All Mine Series:

Senator, Mine

Druid, Mine

Pharaoh, Mine

All Mine: 1Night Stand Collection

Gallant Gentleman's Guild (G3):

Artist's Touch

Sculptor's Desire

Black Hills Wolves Series (shared world, Decadent Publishing):

The Wolf and the Butterfly

The Nightshade Guild (shared world, Celtic Hearts Press):

Midwinter Mage

Magic Masque (October 2022)

Standalone Novels:

Beautiful One

Double Eclipse

Auld Lang Syne

Cruise Control

The Guardian of Blackbird Inn

Saving His Wolf

Ghost in a Bottle (with Lia Davis)

First Contact (with Lia Davis)

Anthologies:

Beefcake m/m authors (Artemis Wolffe)

Unconditional Surrender

Box of 1 Night Stands: 17 Sizzling Nights

Spring Fever: Shifters in Love

Come Undone: Romance Stories Inspired by the Music of Duran Duran

Wicked: Erotic Paranormal Romance Vol 3

Wicked Legends

Starstruck Holidays: A MM Sci-Fi Holiday Romance Anthology

Mated: A Paranormal Romance Shifter Anthology

Scorched: Thirteen Dragon Shifter Paranormal Romance Standalones

ALSO BY L.A. BORUFF

Prime Time of Life (Paranormal Women's Fiction)
COMPLETE SERIES
Series Boxed Set
Complete Series Volume 1
Complete Series Volume 2
Borrowed Time
Stolen Time
Just in Time
Hidden Time
Nick of Time

Witching After Forty (Paranormal Women's Fiction)
A Ghoulish Midlife
Cookies For Satan (*A Christmas Novella*)
I'm With Cupid (*A Valentine's Day Novella*)
A Cursed Midlife
Birthday Blunder
A Girlfriend For Mr. Snoozerton

A Haunting Midlife

An Animated Midlife

Faery Odd Mother

A Killer Midlife

A Grave Midlife

A Powerful Midlife

A Wedded Midlife

Fanged After Forty (Paranormal Women's Fiction)

Bitten in the Midlife

Staked in the Midlife

Masquerading in the Midlife

Bonded in the Midlife

Dominating in the Midlife

Wanted in the Midlife

Magical Midlife in Mystic Hollow (Paranormal Women's Fiction)

Karma's Spell

Karma's Shift

Karma's Spirit

Karma's Sense

Karma's Stake

Karma's Source

Shifting Into Midlife (Paranormal Women's Fiction)

Pack Bunco Night

Alpha Males and Other Shift

The Cat's Meow

Midlife Mage (Paranormal Women's Fiction)

Unfazed

Unbowed

Unsaid

An Immortal Midlife (Paranormal Women's Fiction)

COMPLETE SERIES

Series Boxed Set

Fatal Forty

Fighting Forty

Finishing Forty

Immortal West (Paranormal Women's Fiction)

Undead

Hybrid

Fae

The Meowing Medium (Paranormal Cozy)

COMPLETE SERIES

Series Boxed Set Coming Soon

Secrets of the Specter

Gifts of the Ghost

Pleas of the Poltergeist

An Unseen Midlife (Paranormal Women's Fiction Reverse Harem)

Bloom In Blood

Dance In Night

Bask In Magic

Surrender In Dreams

Tales of Clan Robbins (Paranormal Western Romance)

Outlaw of Ladies

Lady of Outlaws

Princess of Thieves

Alpha of Exiles

The Firehouse Feline (Paranormal Reverse Harem)

COMPLETE SERIES

Series Boxed Set

Feline the Heat

Feline the Flames

Feline the Burn

Feline the Pressure